HOBBIES GNOMIGURUMI

14 Adorable Amigurumi Gnomes to Crochet

Madelenón-Soledad Iglesias Silva

DOVER PUBLICATIONS
Garden City, New York

Hobbies Gnomigurumi: 14 Adorable Amigurumi Gnomes to Crochet
is a new work, first published by Dover Publications in 2026.

ISBN-13: 978-0-486-85524-0
ISBN-10: 0-486-85524-4

Publisher: Betina Cochran
Acquisitions Editor: Allyson D'Antonio
Managing Editorial Supervisor: Susan Rattiner
Production Editor: Gregory Koutrouby
Cover Designer: Peter Donahue
Creative Manager: Marie Zaczkiewicz
Interior Designer: Jennifer Becker
Production: Pam Weston, Tammi McKenna, Ayse Yilmaz

Manufactured in China
85524401 2025
www.doverpublications.com

TABLE OF CONTENTS

Projects

Introduction

When Dover Publications suggested I create a new project about gnomes to follow my previous books, *Flower Gnomigurumi* and *Creepigurumi*, I didn't hesitate. From that first moment, my imagination began to soar. I've always been fascinated by these magical little creatures who seem to hold secrets and lead mysterious lives, and I've wondered how they spend their time. So, little by little, 14 different gnomes took shape—each with a different hobby! Look through the contents and you'll see that some gnomes read, others cook, and still others enjoy crafts, gardening, or sports.

I lovingly brought them together in this book, accompanying each character with clear instructions so everyone can knit them and bring them to life with their own hands.

More than a pattern book, *Hobbies Gnomigurumi* is an invitation to enter a world full of tenderness, color, and fantasy. Each gnome has its own personality, and I'm sure more than one will make you smile, or remind you of someone special.

I hope you enjoy this book as much as I enjoyed creating it.

With love,
Soledad

Abbreviations List

BL: back loop
BL sc: back loop single crochet
ch: chain(s)
dc: double crochet
FL: front loop
FL hdc: front loop half double crochet
FL sc: front loop single crochet
hdc: half double crochet
rnd(s): round(s)
sc: single crochet
sc2tog: single crochet 2 together
sl st: slip stitch
st(s): stitch(es)

BASIC STITCHES

Basic Stitches

Chain (ch)

Make a loop and pull up the yarn through the loop. Pull up the loop until tight. Wrap the yarn over the hook from back to front. Pull the hook, carrying the yarn, through the loop already on your hook. Repeat these steps as many times as indicated.

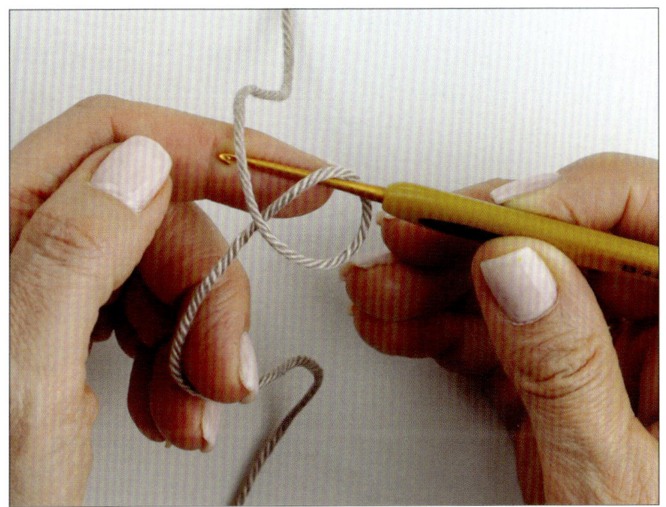

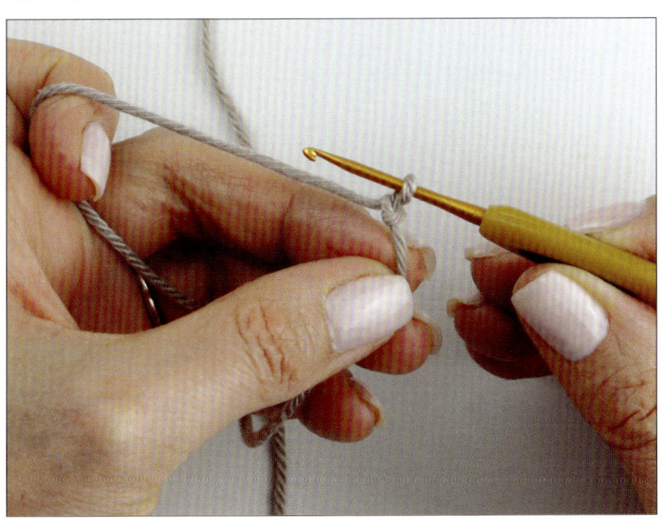

Slip stitch (sl st)

Insert hook in indicated stitch, yarn over, and pull through both loops on hook.

Single Crochet (sc)

Insert hook in indicated stitch, yarn over, and pull through loop, yarn over and pull through both loops on hook.

Magic Ring

Make a loop with your hook, but don't pull it tight. Hold the circle with your index finger and thumb, and wrap the working yarn over your middle finger. Make a chain stitch. Insert the hook into the loop and underneath the tail. Yarn over the hook and draw a loop; yarn over again and pull through both loops on hook. Repeat steps 6, 7, and 8 as many times as indicated. Now grab the yarn tail and pull to draw the center of the ring tightly closed.

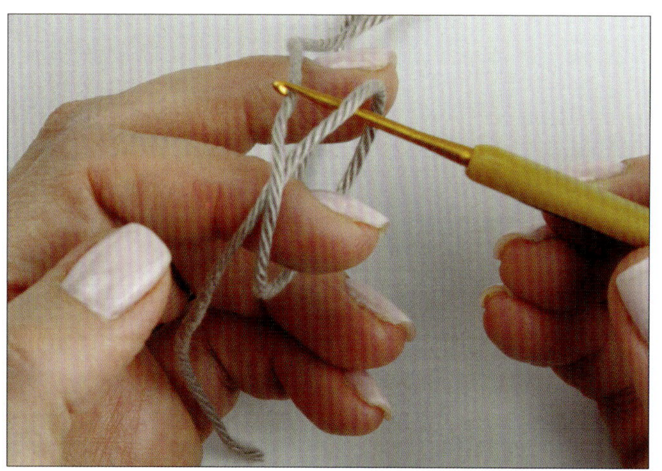

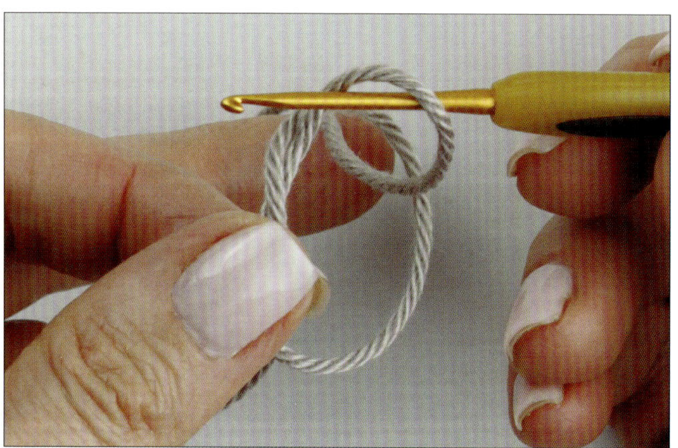

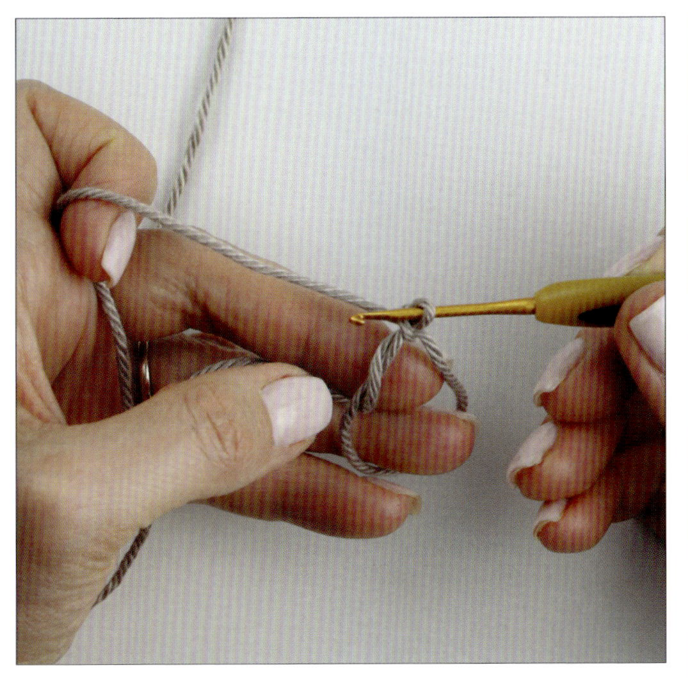

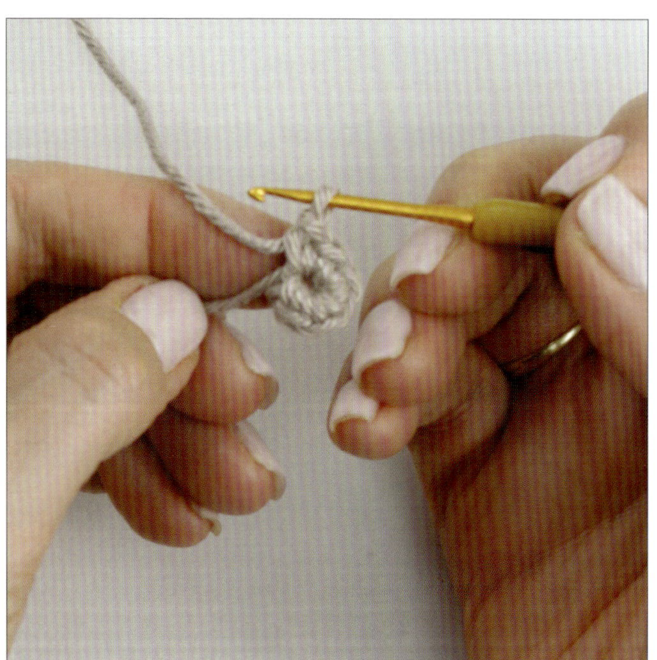

Half Double Crochet (hdc)

Yarn over and insert hook in indicated stitch; yarn over, and pull through loop; yarn over and pull through all 3 loops on hook.

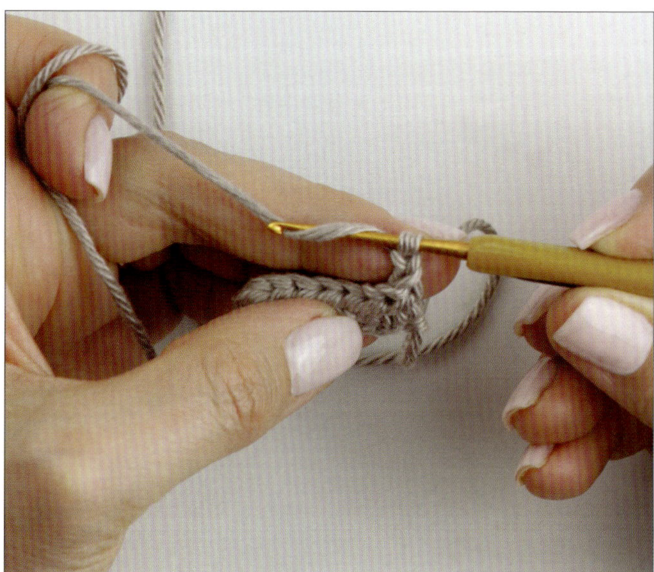

Double Crochet (dc)

Yarn over; insert hook in indicated stitch; yarn over and pull through loop; yarn over and pull through 2 loops twice.

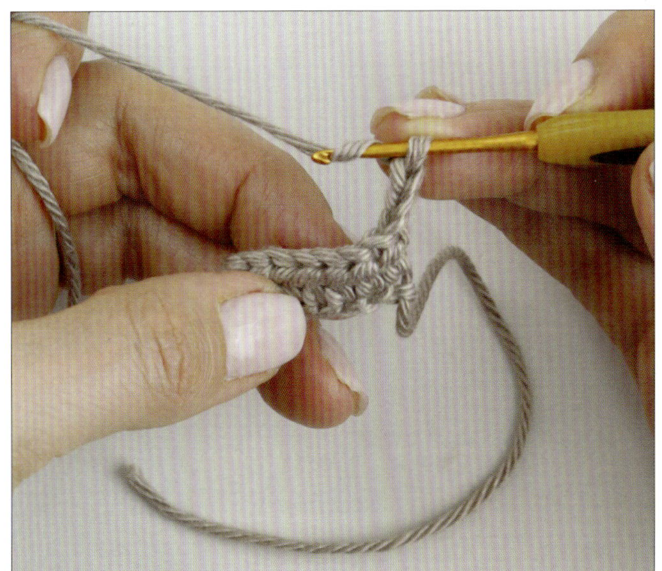

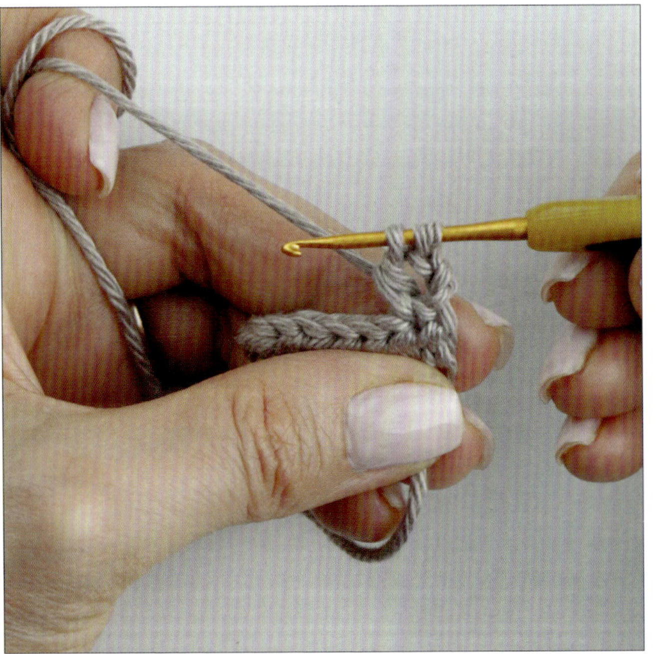

CARPENTRY GNOME

MATERIALS

Yarn

Yarn & Colors® 100% Mercerized Cotton (sport weight yarn) 1.75oz (50g)/137yds (125m)

Colors

Pink Sand: 0.35oz (10g)/27.3yds (25m)
Sorbus: 0.35oz (10g)/27.3yds (25m)
Rose Quartz: 0.35oz (10g)/27.3yds (25m)
Petrol Blue: 0.71oz (20g)/54.7yds (50m)
Brunet: 0.35oz (10g)/27.3yds (25m)
Dark Pink: leftovers
Teak: leftovers
Taupe: 0.35oz (10g)/27.3yds (25m)
Limestone: leftovers
Soft Gray: leftovers

- Size US 0 (2mm) crochet hook (you may need to go up/down based on your tension)
- Fiberfill
- 6mm black safety eyes
- Darning needle
- Locking stitch marker
- Scissors
- Pins
- Skewer stick
- Pompom maker 1.5in/4cm diameter

Gauge

7 stitches x 7 rounds in 1in/2.54cm

Let's Begin!

Hat

With Pink Sand.

Rnd 1: Sc 6 into a MR. (6 sts)

Rnd 2: 2 sc in each st around. (12 sts)

Rnd 3: (Sc 1, sc 2 in next st) x6. (18 sts)

Rnd 4: (Sc 2, sc 2 in next st) x6. (24 sts)

Rnd 5: (Sc 3, sc 2 in next st) x6. (30 sts)

Rnd 6: (Sc 4, sc 2 in next st) x6. (36 sts)

Rnd 7: (Sc 5, sc 2 in next st) x6. (42 sts)

Rnd 8: (Sc 6, sc 2 in next st) x6. (48 sts)

Rnd 9: (Sc 7, sc 2 in next st) x6. (54 sts)

Rnds 10–13: Sc in each st around.

Rnd 14: (Sc 8, sc 2 in next st) x6. (60 sts)

Rnds 15–18: Sc in each st around.

Change to Sorbus.

Rnd 19: (FL hdc 9, FL hdc 2 in next st) x6, sl st in beginning FL hdc to join. (66 sts)

Rnds 20–22: Ch 2, (front post hdc, back post hdc) x33, sl st in beginning ch 2 to join.

Fasten off and weave in the yarn ends. If you wish, sew decorative embroidery.

Head and Robe

With Rose Quartz.

Pull up a loop of Rose Quartz in any BL of Rnd 18 of the hat.

Rnd 1: BL sc in each st around. (60 sts)

Rnd 2: (Sc 8, sc2tog) x6. (54 sts)

Rnd 3: (Sc 7, sc2tog) x6. (48 sts)

Rnds 4–7: Sc each st around.

Change to Petrol Blue.

Rnds 8–11: Sc in each st around.

Rnd 12: (Sc 7, sc 2 in next st) x6. (54 sts)

Rnds 13–16: Sc in each st around.

Place a locking marker in the loop while you make the face.

Position your gnome so that the held loop is centered at the back.

Insert safety eyes between Rnds 3 and 4 of the head, 10 sts apart.

Embroider the cheeks with Dark Pink.

Rnd 17: (Sc 8, sc 2 in next st) x6. (60 sts)

Rnds 18–20: Sc in each st around.

Rnd 21: (FL sc 9, FL sc 2 in next st) x6. (66 sts)

Rnd 22: Sc in each st around.

Rnd 23: (Sc 10, sc 2 in next st) x6. (72 sts)

Rnd 24: Sc in each st around.

Fasten off and weave in the yarn ends.

Bottom

Pull up a loop of Rose Quartz in the BL of any st of Rnd 20 of the robe.

Rnd 1: (BL sc 8, BL sc2tog) x6. (54 sts)

Rnd 2: (Sc 7, sc2tog) x6. (48 sts)

Rnd 3: (Sc 4, sc2tog) x8. (40 sts)

Rnd 4: (Sc 3, sc2tog) x8. (32 sts)

Rnd 5: (Sc 2, sc2tog) x8. (24 sts)

Stuff the body.

Rnd 6: (Sc 1, sc2tog) x8. (16 sts)

Rnd 7: (Sc2tog) x8. (8 sts)

Fasten off, leaving a long tail. Using a darning needle, weave the yarn tail through the FL of each st of the last rnd. Pull tight to close. Weave in the end.

Make a 1in/4cm pompom with Sorbus and sew it to the top of the hat.

Arms (make 2)

With Rose Quartz.

Rnd 1: Sc 6 into a MR. (6 sts)

Rnd 2: Sc 2 in each st around. (12 sts)

Rnds 3–4: Sc in each st around.

Change to Petrol Blue.

Rnds 5–12: Sc in each st around.

Lightly stuff the arm. Flatten the opening at the top of the arm, and work the next row through both layers to close.

Next Round: Sc 5 through both layers, sl st in the last st.

Fasten off, leaving a long tail for sewing.

Nose

With Rose Quartz.

Rnd 1: Sc 6 into a MR. (6 sts)

Rnd 2: Sc 2 in each st around. (12 sts)

Rnd 3: (Sc 1, sc 2 in next st) x6. (18 sts)

Rnd 4: Sc in each st around.

Rnd 5: (Sc 1, sc2tog) x6. (12 sts)

Fasten off, leaving a long tail for sewing.

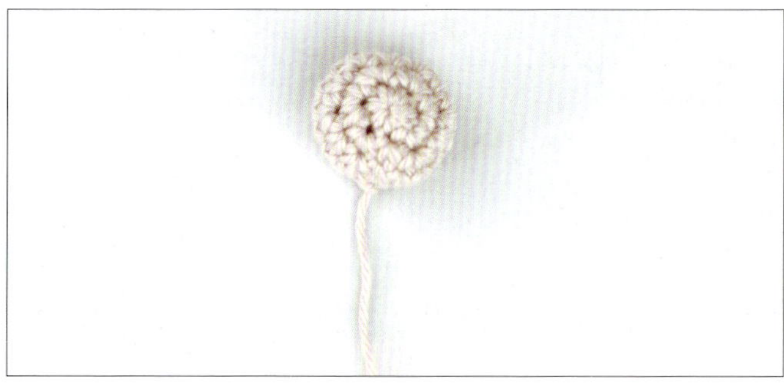

Feet (make 2)

With Teak.

Rnd 1: Sc 6 into a MR. (6 sts)

Rnd 2: Sc 2 in each st around. (12 sts)

Rnds 3–4: Sc in each st around.

The feet don't need to be stuffed. Flatten the opening of the foot and work the next row through both layers to close.

Next Row: Sc 5 through both layers, sl st in the last st.

Fasten off, leaving a long tail for sewing.

Beard

With Brunet.

Start by making 5 parts for the beard, which will be joined together after all are made.

Rnd 1: Sc 5 into a MR. (5 sts)

Rnd 2: Sc 2 in each st around. (10 sts)

Fasten off the first 4 parts. Do not fasten off the fifth part. Continue by joining all the parts.

Rnd 3: Sc 5 along one side of the first part, sc 5 along one side of the second part, sc 5 along one side of the third part, sc 10 around the fourth part, sc 5 st along the remaining side of the third part, sc 5 along the remaining side of the second part, sc 5 along the remaining side of the first part, then sc 10 around the fifth part. (50 sts)

Rnd 4: Sc 4, sc2tog, (sc 3, sc2tog) x3 times, sc 8, sc2tog, (sc 3, sc2tog) x3, sc 4. (42 sts)

Rnd 5: Sc 3, sc2tog, (sc 2, sc2tog) x3, sc 7, sc2tog, (sc 2, sc2tog) x3 times, sc 4. (34 sts)

Rnd 6: (Sc 1, sc2tog) x5, (sc2tog) x2, (sc 1, sc2tog) x5. (22 sts)

Rnd 7: Sc 2, (sc2tog) x3, sc 5, (sc2tog) x3, sc 3. (16 sts)

Rnd 8: (Sc2tog) x8. (8 sts)

The beard doesn't need to be stuffed. Fasten off, leaving a long tail for sewing.

Toolbox

With Taupe.

Ch 15.

Row 1: Sc in the 2nd ch from hook, sc in next 13 ch, ch 1, turn. (14 sts)

Rows 2–5: Sc in st across, ch 1, turn.

Row 6: BL sc in each st across, ch 1, turn.

Rows 7–12: Sc in each st across, ch 1, turn.

Row 13: BL sc in each st across, ch 1, turn.

Rows 14–16: Sc in each st across, ch 1, turn.

Row 17: Sc in each st across.

Fasten off. Weave in the ends.

First Side

Working along the row ends of the toolbox along one side edge, pull up a loop of Taupe in the first st of Row 11.

Rows 1–5: Sc in the next 6 sts, ch 1, turn. (6 sts)

Row 6: Skip the first st, sc in next 5 sts, ch 1, turn. (5 sts)

Row 7: Skip the first st, sc in next 4 sts, ch 1, turn. (4 sts)

Rows 8–11: Sc in each st across, ch 1, turn.

Row 12: Sc in each st across.

Fasten off and weave in the ends.

Second Side

Working along the row ends of the toolbox along the remaining side edge, pull up a loop of Taupe in the first st of Row 6.

Rows 1–5: Sc in the next 6 sts, ch 1, turn. (6 sts)

Row 6: Skip the first st, sc in next 5 sts, ch 1, turn. (5 sts)

Row 7: Skip the first st, sc in next 4 sts, ch 1, turn. (4 sts)

Rows 8–11: Sc in next 4 sts, ch 1, turn.

Row 12: Sc in each st across.

Fasten off and weave in the ends.

Match the sts of Rows 1–5 as well as possible and sew the edges of the tool box to the sides of the handles.

To make the toolbox handle, cut a piece of skewer approximately 3.15in/8cm long and insert it into both sides of the toolbox between Rows 11 and 12.

Saw

With Soft Gray.

Ch 5.

Rnd 1: Sc in the 2nd ch from hook, sc in next 3 ch, continue along the other side of the foundation ch, sc in next 4 ch. (8 sts)

Rnds 2–3: Sc in each st around.

Rnd 4: (Sc 3, sc 2 in next st) x2. (10 sts)

Rnd 5: Sc in each st around.

Rnd 6: Sc 4, sc 2 in next st, sc 5. (11 sts)

Rnd 7: Sc 5, sc 2 in next st, sc 5. (12 sts)

Rnd 8: Sc 6, sc 2 in next st, sc 5. (13 sts)

Rnd 9: Sc 6, sc 2 in next st, sc 6. (14 sts)

Rnd 10: Sc 7, sc 2 in next st, sc 6. (15 sts)

Rnd 11: Sc in each st around.

Rnd 12: Sc 8, sc 2 in next st, sc 6. (16 sts)

Rnds 13–14: Sc in each st around.

Rnd 15: Sc in each st around, then sc 3 st to reach the edge of the saw.

Change to Limestone.

Rnd 16: Sc in each st around.

Flatten the opening of the saw and work the next round through both layers to close.

Next Row: Sc in 8 through both layers. (8 sts)

Next 2 Rows: Ch 1, turn, sc 2. (2 sts)

Next Row: Ch 1, turn, sc 2, ch 6. (2 sts + 6 ch)

Next Row: Skip next 4 sts along the joined edge, sc in next 2 sts. (2 sts)

Next Row: Ch 1, turn, skip the first st, sc in next st, sc 6 along the ch, then sc 2 in the last 2 sts.

Fasten off and weave in ends.

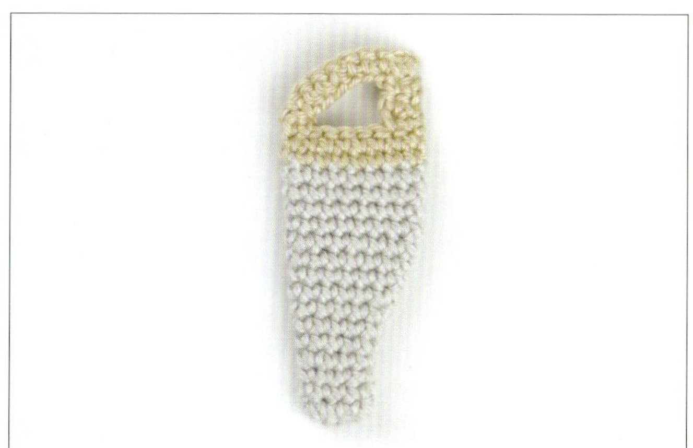

Hammer

With Soft Gray.

Ch 7, leaving a long tail for sewing.

Row 1: Sc in the 2nd ch from hook, sc in next 5 ch, ch 1, turn. (6 sts)

Row 2: Sc in each st across, ch 1, turn.

Row 3: BL sc in each st across, ch 1, turn.

Row 4: Sc in each st across, ch 1, turn.

Row 5: BL sc in each st across, ch 1, turn.

Row 6: Sc in each st across, ch 1, turn.

Row 7: BL sc in each st across, ch 1, turn.

Row 8: Sc in each st across.

Row 9: Fold the hammer with Rows 1 and 8 together, working through both layers, sl st in each st across.

Do not cut the yarn.

Next Rnd: Work in the row ends, ch 1, sc 8 along the side edge.

Fasten off, leaving a long tail. Using a darning needle, weave the yarn tail through the FL of each st of the last rnd. Pull tight to close. Weave in the end. Flatten the other side of the hammer. Using a darning needle and long tail from the beginning ch, sew the remaining edges closed. Weave in the end.

Cut 1.5in/4cm from the pointed tip of a skewer stick for the handle, put a drop of glue on the pointed end of the handle and insert it into the hammer.

Time to Put It All Together!

Sew the beard, centered between the eyes and between Rnds 5 and 7 of the head.

Stuff the nose and sew it to the head, centered above the beard and between Rnds 3 and 7 of the head.

Sew the arms to the sides of the robe on Rnd 8 of the body, with 22 sts between them at the back.

Sew the feet to Rnd 1 at the bottom of the body, with 6 sts between them at the front.

COOKiNG GNOME

MATERIALS

Yarn

Yarn & Colors® 100% Mercerized Cotton (sport weight yarn) 1.75oz (50g)/137yds (125m)

Colors

White: 1.06oz (30g)/82yds (75m)
Rose Quartz: 0.35oz (10g)/27.3yds (25m)
Cardinal: 0.71oz (20g)/54.7yds (50m)
Dark Pink: leftovers
Teak: leftovers
Satay: leftovers
Limestone: leftovers

- Size US 0 (2mm) crochet hook (you may need to go up/down based on your tension)
- Fiberfill
- 6mm black safety eyes
- Darning needle
- Locking stitch marker
- Scissors
- Pins

Gauge

7 stitches x 7 rounds in 1in/2.54cm

Let's Begin!

Hat

With White.

Rnd 1: Sc 6 sc into a MR. (6 sts)

Rnd 2: Sc 2 in each st around. (12 sts)

Rnd 3: (Sc 1, sc 2 in next st) x6. (18 sts)

Rnd 4: (Sc 2, sc 2 in next st) x6. (24 sts)

Rnd 5: (Sc 3, sc 2 in next st) x6. (30 sts)

Rnd 6: (Sc 4, sc 2 in next st) x6. (36 sts)

Rnd 7: (Sc 5, sc 2 in next st) x6. (42 sts)

Rnd 8: (Sc 6, sc 2 in next st) x6. (48 sts)

Rnd 9: (Sc 7, sc 2 in next st) x6. (54 sts)

Rnd 10: (Sc 8, sc 2 in next st) x6. (60 sts)

Rnd 11: (Sc 9, sc 2 in next st) x6. (66 sts)

Rnd 12: (Sc 10, sc 2 in next st) x6. (72 sts)

Rnd 13: (Sc 11, sc 2 in next st) x6. (78 sts)

Rnd 14: (Sc 12, sc 2 in next st) x6. (84 sts)

Rnd 15: (Sc 13, sc 2 in next st) x6. (90 sts)

Rnd 16: (Sc 1, sc 2 in next st) x45. (135 sts)

Rnds 17–24: Sc in each st around.

Rnd 25: (Sc 1, sc2tog) x45. (90 sts)

Rnd 26: (Sc2tog) x45. (45 sts)

Rnds 27–32: Sc in each st around.

Rnd 33: (Sc 14, sc 2 in next st) x3. (48 sts)

Rnd 34: (Sc 7, sc 2 in next st) x6. (54 sts)

Rnd 35: (Sc 8, sc 2 in next st) x6. (60 sts)

Rnd 36: (FL sc 9, FL sc 2 in next st) x6. (66 sts)

Rnd 37: Sc in each st around.

Rnd 38: (Sc 10, sc 2 in next st) x6. (72 sts)

Rnd 39: Sc in each st around.

Fasten off and weave in the yarn ends.

Head and Robe

With Rose Quartz.

Pull up a loop of Rose Quartz in any BL of Rnd 35 of the hat.

Rnd 1: BL sc in each st around. (60 sts)

Rnd 2: (Sc 8, sc2tog) x6. (54 sts)

Rnd 3: (Sc 7, sc2tog) x6. (48 sts)

Rnds 4–7: Sc in each st around.

Change to Cardinal.

Rnds 8–11: Sc in each st around.

Rnd 12: (Sc 7, sc 2 in next st) x6. (54 sts)

Rnds 13–16: Sc in each st around.

Place a locking marker in the loop while you make the face.

Position your gnome so that the held loop is centered at the back.

Insert safety eyes between Rnds 3 and 4 of the head, 10 sts apart.

Embroider the cheeks with Dark Pink.

Rnd 17: (Sc 8, sc 2 in next st) x6. (60 sts)

Rnds 18–20: Sc in each st around.

Rnd 21: (FL sc 9, FL sc 2 in next st) x6. (66 sts)

Rnd 22: Sc in each st around.

Rnd 23: (Sc 10, sc 2 in next st) x6. (72 sts)

Rnd 24: Sc in each st around.

Fasten off and weave in the yarn ends.

Bottom

Pull up a loop of Rose Quartz in the BL of any st of Rnd 20 of the robe.

Rnd 1: (BL sc 8, BL sc2tog) x6. (54 sts)

Rnd 2: (Sc 7, sc2tog) x6. (48 sts)

Rnd 3: (Sc 4, sc2tog) x8. (40 sts)

Rnd 4: (Sc 3, sc2tog) x8. (32 sts)

Rnd 5: (Sc 2, sc2tog) x8. (24 sts)

Stuff the body.

Rnd 6: (Sc 1, sc2tog) x8. (16 sts)

Rnd 7: (Sc2tog) x8. (8 sts)

Fasten off, leaving a long tail. Using a darning needle, weave the yarn tail through the FL of each st of the last rnd. Pull it tight to close. Weave in the end.

Arms (make 2)

With Rose Quartz.

Rnd 1: Sc 6 into a MR. (6 sts)

Rnd 2: Sc 2 in each st around. (12 sts)

Rnds 3–4: Sc in each st around.

Change to Cardinal.

Rnds 5–12: Sc in each st around.

Lightly stuff the arm. Flatten the opening of the arm and work the next row through both layers to close.

Next Row: Sc 5 through both layers, sl st in last st.

Fasten off, leaving a long tail for sewing.

Nose

With Rose Quartz.

Rnd 1: Sc 6 sc into a MR. (6 sts)

Rnd 2: Sc 2 in each st around. (12 sts)

Rnd 3: (Sc 1, sc 2 in next st) x6. (18 sts)

Rnd 4: Sc in each st around.

Rnd 5: (Sc 1, sc2tog) x6. (12 sts)

Fasten off, leaving a long tail for sewing.

Feet (make 2)

With Teak.

Rnd 1: Sc 6 into a MR. (6 sts)

Rnd 2: Sc 2 in each st around. (12 sts)

Rnds 3–4: Sc in each st around.

The feet don't need to be stuffed. Flatten the opening of the foot and work the next row through both layers to close.

Next Row: Sc 5 through both layers, sl st in last st.

Fasten off, leaving a long tail for sewing.

Mustaches (make 2)

With Satay.

Ch 7.

Rnd 1: Sl st in 2nd ch from hook, sc 2 in next ch, hdc in next ch, dc in next ch, hdc in next ch, sc in next ch.

Fasten off, leaving a long tail for sewing.

Apron

With White.

Row 1: Sc 5 into a MR, ch 1, turn. (5 sts)

Row 2: Sc 2 in each st across, ch 1, turn. (10 sts)

Row 3: (Sc 1, sc 2 in next st) x5, ch 1, turn. (15 sts)

Row 4: (Sc 2, sc 2 in next st) x5 times, ch 1, don't turn. (20 sts)

Row 5: Sc 8 along top edge, ch 48. Fasten off and leave a yarn tail.

Place the apron at Rnd 14 of the robe, pass the ch around the body and secure then end of the ch with a few sts to the other side of the apron. Weave in the yarn ends.

Spoon

With Limestone.

Rnd 1: Sc 6 into a MR. (6 sts)

Rnd 2: Sc 2 in each st around. (12 sts)

Rnd 3: (Sc 1, sc 2 in next st) x6. (18 sts)

Rnds 4–9: Sc in each st around.

Rnd 10: (Sc 1, sc2tog) x6. (12 sts)

Rnd 11: (Sc2tog) x6. (6 sts)

Rnds 12–25: Sc in each st around.

Fasten off, leaving a long tail. Using a darning needle, weave the yarn tail through the FL of each st of the last rnd. Pull tight to close. Weave in the yarn end.

Time to Put It All Together!

Sew the mustaches, centered between the eyes and between Rnds 5 and 7 of the head, with 4 sts between them.

Stuff the nose and sew it to the head, centered between the mustaches and between Rnds 3 and 7 of the head.

Sew the arms to the sides of the robe, on Rnd 8 and with 22 sts between them at the back.

Sew the feet to Rnd 1 at the bottom of the body, with 6 sts between them at the front.

Sew the spoon to his hand.

FISHING GNOME

MATERIALS

Yarn

Yarn & Colors® 100% Mercerized Cotton (sport weight yarn) 1.75oz (50g)/137yds (125m)

Colors

Taupe: 0.71oz (20g)/54.7yds (50m)
Coral: leftovers
Limestone: 0.35oz (10g)/27.3yds (25m)
Satay: leftovers
Olive: 1.06oz (30g)/82yds (75m)
Dark Pink: leftovers
Grape: leftovers
Cream: leftovers
Teak: leftovers

- Size US 0 (2mm) crochet hook (you may need to go up/down based on your tension)
- Fiberfill
- 6mm black safety eyes
- Darning needle
- Locking stitch marker
- Scissors
- Pins
- Twig
- 2 tiny black beads
- Black thread and sewing needle

Gauge

7 stitches x 7 rounds in 1in/2.54cm

Let's Begin!

Hat

With Taupe.

Rnd 1: Sc 6 into a MR. (6 sts)

Rnd 2: Sc 2 in each st around. (12 sts)

Rnd 3: (Sc 1, sc 2 in next st) x6. (18 sts)

Rnd 4: (Sc 2, sc 2 in next st) x6. (24 sts)

Rnd 5: (Sc 3, sc 2 in next st) x6. (30 sts)

Rnd 6: (Sc 4, sc 2 in next st) x6. (36 sts)

Rnd 7: (Sc 5, sc 2 in next st) x6. (42 sts)

Rnd 8: (Sc 6, sc 2 in next st) x6. (48 sts)

Rnd 9: (Sc 7, sc 2 in next st) x6. (54 sts)

Rnds 10–13: Sc in each st around.

Rnd 14: (Sc 8, sc 2 in next st) x6. (60 sts)

Rnd 15: Sc in each st around.

Change to Coral.

Rnd 16: FL sc in each st around.

Rnds 17–18: Sc in each st around.

Change to Taupe.

Rnd 19: (FL sc 9, FL sc 2 in next st) x6. (66 sts)

Rnd 20: (Sc 10, sc 2 in next st) x6. (72 sts)

Rnd 21: Sc 6, sc 2 in next st, (sc 11, sc 2 in next st) x5, sc 5. (78 sts)

Rnd 22: (Sc 12, sc 2 in next st) x6. (84 sts)

Rnd 23: Sc in each st around.

Fasten off and weave in the yarn ends.

Head and Robe

With Limestone.

Pull up a loop in any BL of Rnd 15 of the hat.

Rnd 1: BL sc in next 17 sts of Rnd 15, BL sc in next 26 sts of Rnd 18, then BL sc in next 17 sts of Rnd 15. (60 sts)

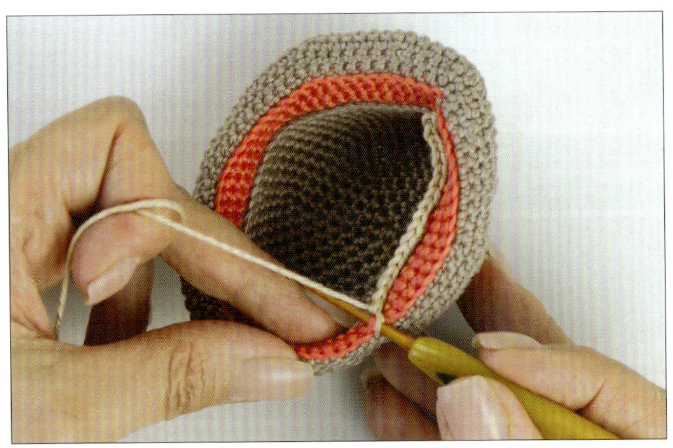

Rnd 2: (Sc 8, sc2tog) x6. (54 sts)

Rnd 3: (Sc 7, sc2tog) x6. (48 sts)

Rnds 4–7: Sc in each st around.

Change to Olive.

Rnds 8–11: Sc in each st around.

Rnd 12: (Sc 7, sc 2 in next st) x6. (54 sts)

Rnds 13–16: Sc in each st around.

Place a locking marker in the loop while you make the face.

Position your gnome so that the held loop is centered at the back.

Insert safety eyes between Rnds 3 and 4 of the head, 10 sts apart.

Embroider the cheeks with Dark Pink.

Rnd 17: (Sc 8, sc 2 in next st) x6. (60 sts)

Rnds 18–20: Sc in each st around.

Rnd 21: (FL sc 9, FL sc 2 in next st) x6. (66 sts)

Rnd 22: Sc in each st around.

Rnd 23: (Sc 10, sc 2 in next st) x6. (72 sts)

Rnd 24: Sc in each st around.

Fasten off and weave in the yarn ends.

Bottom

Pull up a loop of Limestone in the BL of any st of Rnd 20 of the robe.

Rnd 1: (BL sc 8, BL sc2tog) x6. (54 sts)

Rnd 2: (Sc 7, sc2tog) x6. (48 sts)

Rnd 3: (Sc 4, sc2tog) x8. (40 sts)

Rnd 4: (Sc 3, sc2tog) x8. (32 sts)

Rnd 5: (Sc 2, sc2tog) x8. (24 sts)

Stuff the body.

Rnd 6: (Sc 1, sc2tog) x8. (16 sts)

Rnd 7: (Sc2tog) x8. (8 sts)

Fasten off, leaving a long tail. Using a darning needle, weave the yarn tail through the FL of each st of the last rnd. Pull tight to close. Weave in the end.

Arms (make 2)

With Limestone.

Rnd 1: Sc 6 into a MR. (6 sts)

Rnd 2: Sc 2 in each st around. (12 sts)

Rnds 3–4: Sc in each st around.

Change to Olive.

Rnds 5–12: Sc in each st around.

Lightly stuff the arm. Flatten the opening at the top of the arm, and work the next row through both layers to close.

Next Row: Sc 5 through both layers, sl st in the last st.

Fasten off, leaving a long tail for sewing.

Nose

With Limestone.

Rnd 1: Sc 6 into a MR. (6 sts)

Rnd 2: Sc 2 in each st around. (12 sts)

Rnd 3: (Sc 1, sc 2 in next st) x6. (18 sts)

Rnd 4: Sc in each st around.

Rnd 5: (Sc 1, sc2tog) x6. (12 sts)

Fasten off, leaving a long tail for sewing.

Feet (make 2)

With Teak.

Rnd 1: Sc 6 into a MR. (6 sts)

Rnd 2: Sc 2 in each st around. (12 sts)

Rnds 3–4: Sc in each st around.

The feet don't need to be stuffed. Flatten the opening of the foot and work the next row through both layers to close.

Rnd 5: Sc 5 through both layers, sl st in the last st.

Fasten off, leaving a long tail for sewing.

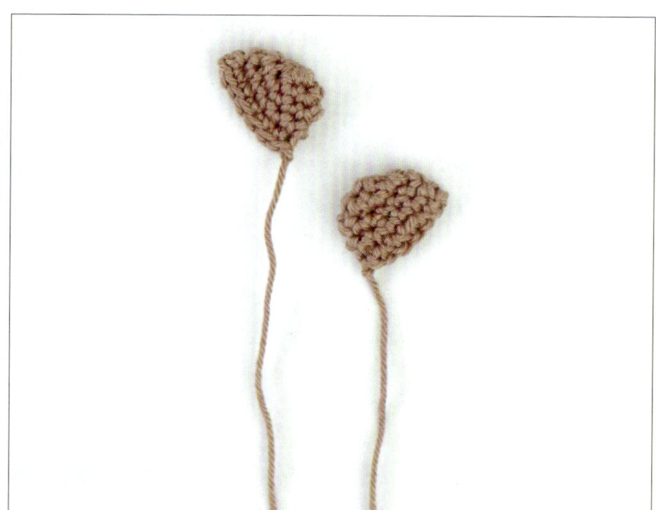

Beard

With Satay.

Rnd 1: Sc 6 into a MR. (6 sts)

Rnd 2: Sc in each st around.

Rnd 3: (Sc 1, sc 2 in next st) x3. (9 sts)

Rnd 4: Hdc 2 in next st, sc 8. (10 sts)

Rnd 5: Hdc 2 in next st, hdc 1, sc 2, hdc 1, hdc 2 in next st, hdc 1, sc 2, hdc 1. (12 sts)

Rnd 6: (Sc 1, sc 2 in next st) x6. (18 sts)

Rnd 7: (Sc 2 in next st, sc 8) x2. (20 sts)

Rnd 8: (Sc 3, sc 2 in next st) x5. (25 sts)

Rnd 9: Sc in each st around.

Rnd 10: (Sc 4, sc 2 in next st) x5. (30 sts)

Rnd 11: (Sc 2 in next st, sc 14) x2. (32 sts)

The beard doesn't need to be stuffed. Flatten the opening of the beard and work the next row through both layers to close.

Next Row: Sc 15 through both layers, sl st in the last st.

Fasten off, leaving a long tail for sewing.

Mustaches (make 2)

With Satay.

Ch 7.

Rnd 1: Sl st in 2nd ch from the hook, sc 2 in next ch, hdc in next ch, dc in next ch, hdc in next ch, sc in next ch.

Fasten off, leaving a long tail for sewing.

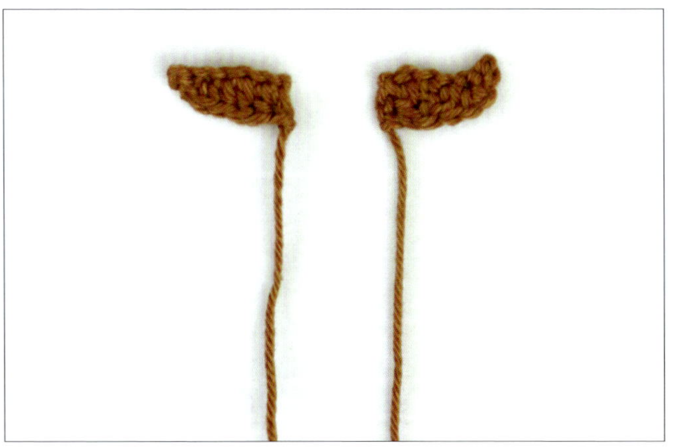

Fish

With Grape.

Rnd 1: Sc 6 into a MR. (6 sts)

Rnd 2: (Sc 1, sc 2 in next st) x3. (9 sts)

Rnd 3: Sc in each st around.

Rnd 4: (Sc 2, sc 2 in next st) x3. (12 sts)

Rnd 5: (Sc 3, sc 2 in next st) x3. (15 sts)

Rnds 6–7: Sc in each st around.

Rnd 8: (Sc 3, sc2tog) x3. (12 sts)

Stuff lightly.

Rnd 9: (Sc2tog) x6. (6 sts)

Flatten the opening of the fish and work the next row through both layers to close.

Next Row: Sl st 1 through both layers, ch 3, dc 6 in next st, ch 3, sl st in the last st.

Fasten off and weave in the yarn ends.

Sew the black beads to the sides of the fish's body to make the eyes. Tie one end of the piece of cream-colored yarn to the twig and attach the fish to the other end.

Time to Put It All Together!

Sew the beard, centered between the eyes, at Rnd 7 of the head.

Sew the mustaches to the beard, with 4 sts between them.

Stuff the nose and sew it to the head, centered between the eyes and between Rnds 3 and 7 of the head.

Sew the arms to the sides of the robe, at Rnd 8, with 22 sts between them at the back.

Sew the feet to Rnd 1 at the bottom of the body, with 6 sts between them at the front.

GARDENING GNOME

MATERIALS

Yarn

Yarn & Colors® 100% Mercerized Cotton (sport weight yarn) 1.75oz (50g)/137yds (125m)

Colors

Mustard: 1.06oz (30g)/82yds (75m)
Clay: 0.35oz (10g)/27.3yds (25m)
Petrol Blue: 1.06oz (30g)/82yds (75m)
White: 1.06oz (30g)/82yds (75m)
Teak: leftovers
Dark Pink: leftovers
Cantaloupe: leftovers
Sunflower: leftovers
Black: leftovers

- Size US 0 (2mm) crochet hook (you may need to go up/down based on your tension)
- Fiberfill
- 6mm black safety eyes
- Darning needle
- Locking stitch marker
- Scissors
- Pins

Gauge

7 stitches x 7 rounds in 1in/2.54cm

Let's Begin!

Hat

With Mustard.

Rnd 1: Sc 6 into a MR. (6 sts)

Rnds 2–3: Sc each st around.

Rnd 4: Sc 5, sc 2 in next st. (7 sts)

Rnd 5: Sc 6, sc 2 in next st. (8 sts)

Rnd 6: Sc 7, sc 2 in next st. (9 sts)

Rnd 7: Sc 8, sc 2 in next st. (10 sts)

Rnd 8: Sc 9, sc 2 in next st. (11 sts)

Rnd 9: Sc 10, sc 2 in next st. (12 sts)

Rnd 10: Sc in each st around.

Rnd 11: (Sc 2, sc 2 in next st) x4. (16 sts)

Rnd 12: Sc in each st around.

Rnd 13: (Sc 1, sc 2 in next st) x8. (24 sts)

Rnds 14–17: Sc in each st around.

Rnd 18: (Sc 2, sc 2 in next st) x8. (32 sts)

Rnds 19–20: Sc in each st around.

Rnd 21: (Sc 3, sc 2 in next st) x8. (40 sts)

Rnd 22: (Sc 9, sc 2 in next st) x4. (44 sts)

Rnd 23: (Sc 10, sc 2 in next st) x4. (48 sts)

Rnd 24: Sc in each st around.

Rnd 25: (Sc 7, sc 2 in next st) x6. (54 sts)

Rnd 26: Sc in each st around.

Rnd 27: (Sc 8, sc 2 in next st) x6. (60 sts)

Rnds 28–29: Sc in each st around.

Rnd 30: (FL sc 9, FL sc 2 in next st) x6. (66 sts)

Rnd 31: Sc in each st around.

Rnd 32: (Sc 10, sc 2 in next st) x6. (72 sts)

Rnd 33: Sc in each st around.

Fasten off and weave in the yarn ends. Cut 36 pieces of yarn for fringes, each approximately 2in (5cm) long. Fold one strand in half, insert your hook into any st of the last round of the hat, pull the yarn halfway through, then pull both ends through the loop and tighten to make a knot. Continue attaching a fringe to every other st along the last round. Trim the ends.

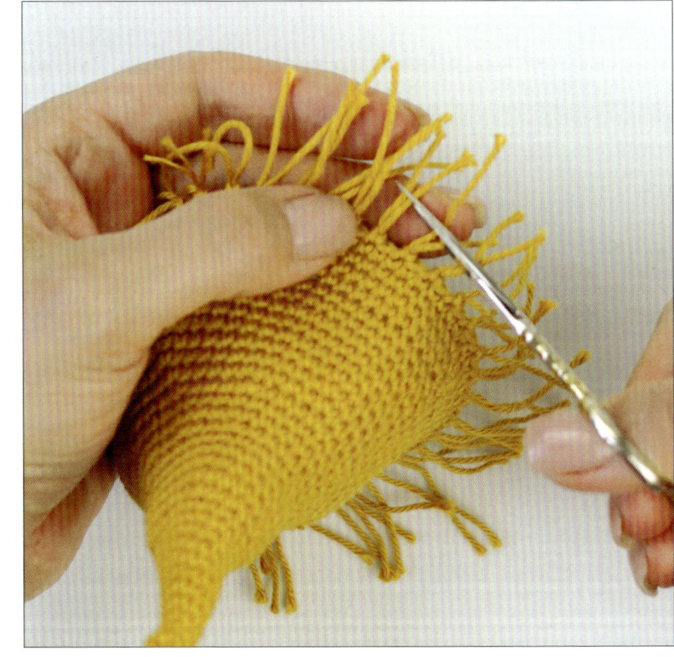

Head and Robe

With Clay.

Pull up a loop of Clay in any BL of Rnd 29 of the hat.

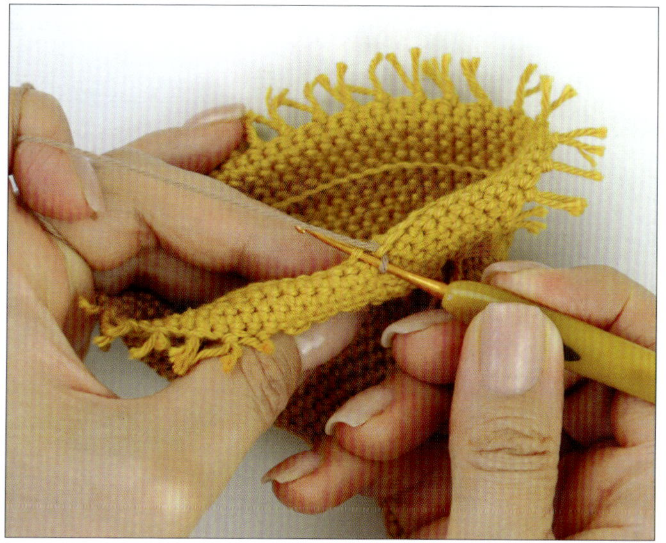

Rnd 1: BL sc in in each st around. (60 sts)

Rnd 2: (Sc 8, sc2tog) x6. (54 sts)

Rnd 3: (Sc 7, sc2tog) x6. (48 sts)

Rnds 4–7: Sc in each st around.

Change to Petrol Blue.

Rnds 8–11: Sc in each st around.

Rnd 12: (Sc 7, sc 2 in next st) x6. (54 sts)

Rnds 13–16: Sc in each st around.

Place a locking marker in the loop while you make the face.

Position your gnome so that the held loop is centered at the back.

Insert the safety eyes between Rnds 3 and 4 of the head, 10 sts apart.

Embroider the cheeks with Dark Pink.

Rnd 17: (Sc 8, sc 2 in next st) x6. (60 sts)

Rnds 18–20: Sc in each st around.

Rnd 21: (FL sc 9, FL sc 2 in next st) x6. (66 sts)

Rnd 22: Sc in each st around.

Rnd 23: (Sc 10, sc 2 in next st) x6. (72 sts)

Rnd 24: Sc in each st around.

Bottom

Pull up a loop of Clay in the BL of any st of Rnd 20 of the robe.

Rnd 1: (BL sc 8, BL sc2tog) x6. (54 sts)

Rnd 2: (Sc 7, sc2tog) x6. (48 sts)

Rnd 3: (Sc4, sc2tog) x8. (40 sts)

Rnd 4: (Sc 3, sc2tog) x8. (32 sts)

Rnd 5: (Sc 2, sc2tog) x8. (24 sts)

Stuff the body.

Rnd 6: (Sc 1, sc2tog) x8. (16 sts)

Rnd 7: (Sc2tog) x8. (8 sts)

Fasten off, leaving a long tail. Using a darning needle, weave the yarn tail through the FL of each st of the last rnd. Pull tight to close. Weave in the yarn end.

Arms (make 2)

With Clay.

Rnd 1: Sc 6 into a MR. (6 sts)

Rnd 2: Sc 2 in each st around. (12 sts)

Rnds 3–4: Sc in each st around.

Change to Petrol Blue.

Rnds 5–12: Sc in each st around.

Lightly stuff the arm. Flatten the opening at the top of the arm and work the next row through both layers to close.

Next Row: Sc 5 through both layers, sl st in the last st.

Fasten off, leaving a long tail for sewing.

Nose

With Clay.

Rnd 1: Sc 6 into a MR. (6 sts)

Rnd 2: Sc 2 in each st around. (12 sts)

Rnd 3: (Sc 1, sc 2 in next st) x6. (18 sts)

Rnd 4: Sc in each st around.

Rnd 5: (Sc 1, sc2tog) x6. (12 sts)

Fasten off, leaving a long tail for sewing.

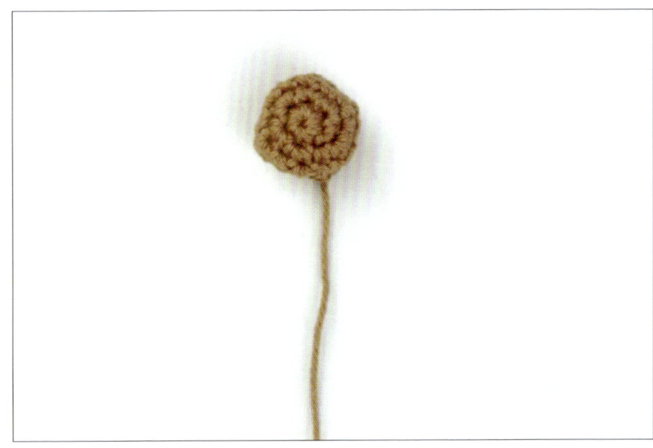

Feet (make 2)

With Teak.

Rnd 1: Sc 6 into a MR. (6 sts)

Rnd 2: Sc 2 in each st around. (12 sts)

Rnds 3–4: Sc in each st around.

The feet don't need to be stuffed. Flatten the opening of the foot and work the next row through both layers to close.

Rnd 5: Sc 5 through both layers, sl st in the last st.

Fasten off, leaving a long tail for sewing.

Beard

With White.

Start by making 5 parts for the beard, which will be joined together after all are made.

Rnd 1: Sc 5 into a MR. (5 sts)

Rnd 2: Sc 2 in each st around. (10 sts)

Fasten off on the first 4 parts. Do not fasten off the fifth part. Continue by joining all the parts.

Rnd 3: Sc 5 along one side of the first part, sc 5 along one side of the second part, sc 5 along one side of the third part, sc 10 around the fourth part, sc 5 st along the remaining side of the third part, sc 5 along the remaining side of the second part, sc 5 along the remaining side of the first part, then sc 10 around the fifth part. (50 sts)

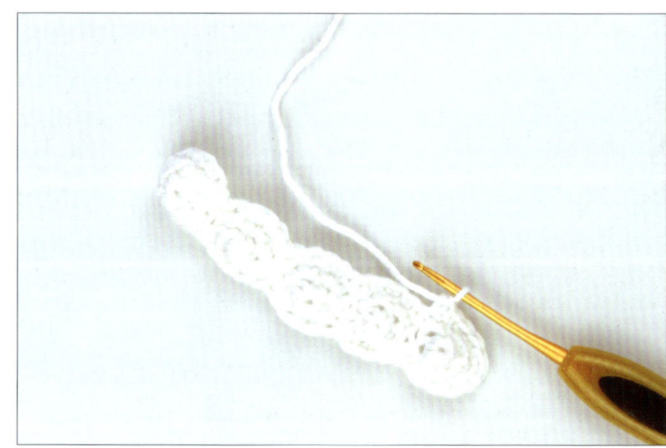

Rnd 4: Sc 4, sc2tog, (sc 3, sc2tog) x3, sc 8, sc2tog, (sc 3, sc2tog) x3, sc 4. (42 sts)

Rnd 5: Sc 3, sc2tog, (sc 2, sc2tog) x3, sc 7, sc2tog, (sc 2, sc2tog) x3, sc 4. (34 sts)

Rnd 6: (Sc 1, sc2tog) x5, (sc2tog) x2, (sc 1, sc2tog) x5. (22 sts)

Rnd 7: Sc 2, (sc2tog) x3, sc 5, (sc2tog) x3, sc 3. (16 sts)

Rnd 8: (Sc2tog) x8. (8 sts)

The beard doesn't need to be stuffed. Fasten off, leaving a long tail for sewing.

Patches (make 2)

One with Cantaloupe and one with Sunflower.

Ch 5.

Row 1: Sc in 2nd ch from the hook, sc in next 3 ch, ch 1, turn. (4 sts)

Rows 2–3: Sc 4, ch 1, turn.

Row 4: Sc 4.

Fasten off and weave in the yarn ends.

Shovel

With Cantaloupe.

Ch 11.

Rnd 1: Sc in 2nd ch from hook, then sc in next 9 ch, continue along the other side of the foundation ch, sc in next 10 sts. (20 sts)

Rnds 2–9: Sc in each st around.

Rnd 10: (Sc 3, sc2tog) x4. (16 sts)

Rnd 11: (Sc 2, sc2tog) x4. (12 sts)

Rnd 12: (Sc2tog) x6. (6 sts)

Rnds 13–29: Sc in each st around.

The shovel doesn't need to be stuffed. Fasten off, leaving a yarn tail. Using a darning needle, weave the yarn tail through the FL of each st of the last rnd. Pull tight to close. Weave in the yarn end.

Time to Put It All Together!

Sew the patches to the robe between Rnds 13 and 20. Make decorative sts around each patch with Black.

Sew the beard, centered between the eyes and between Rnds 5 and 7 of the head.

Stuff the nose and sew it to the head, centered between the eyes and between Rnds 3 and 7 of the head.

Sew the arms to the sides of the robe, on Rnd 8 with 22 sts between them at the back.

Sew the feet to Rnd 1 at the bottom of the body, with 6 sts between them at the front.

GOLFiNG GNOME

MATERIALS

Yarn

Yarn & Colors® 100% Mercerized Cotton (sport weight yarn) 1.75oz (50g)/137yds (125m)

Colors

Aventurine: 0.35oz (10g)/27.3yds (25m)
Limestone: 0.35oz (10g)/27.3yds (25m)
Lettuce: 0.71oz (20g)/54.7yds (50m)
Dark Pink: leftovers
Teak: leftovers
White: leftovers
Brunet: leftovers
Black: leftovers

- Size US 0 (2mm) crochet hook (you may need to go up/down based on your tension)
- Fiberfill
- 6mm black safety eyes
- Darning needle
- Locking stitch marker
- Scissors
- Pins
- Skewer stick
- Black permanent marker

Gauge

7 stitches x 7 rounds in 1in/2.54cm

Let's Begin!

Cap

With Aventurine.

Rnd 1: Sc 6 into a MR. (6 sts)

Rnd 2: Sc 2 in each st around. (12 sts)

Rnd 3: (Sc 1, sc 2 in next st) x6. (18 sts)

Rnd 4: (Sc 2, sc 2 in next st) x6. (24 sts)

Rnd 5: (Sc 3, sc 2 in next st) x6. (30 sts)

Rnd 6: (Sc 4, sc 2 in next st) x6. (36 sts)

Rnd 7: (Sc 5, sc 2 in next st) x6. (42 sts)

Rnd 8: (Sc 6, sc 2 in next st) x6. (48 sts)

Rnd 9: (Sc 7, sc 2 in next st) x6. (54 sts)

Rnds 10–13: Sc in each st around.

Rnd 14: (Sc 8, sc 2 in next st) x6. (60 sts)

Rnd 15: Sc in each st around.

Rnd 16: FL sc in each st around.

Rnds 17–18: Sc in each st around.

Row 1: FL sc 21, ch 1, turn. (21 sts)

Row 2: Sc 4, (sc 2 in next st, sc 2) x4, sc 2 in next st, sc 4, ch 1, turn. (26 sts)

Row 3: Skip first st, sc in next 23 sts, skip 1 st, sc in next st, ch 1, turn. (24 sts)

Row 4: Skip first st, sc in next 21 sts, skip 1 st, sc in next st. (22 sts)

Fasten off and weave in the yarn ends.

Pull up a loop of Aventurine in the center st of Rnd 18 at the back of the cap. Work 1 rnd of sc along the entire edge of the edge of the cap. Fasten off and weave in the yarn ends.

Head and Robe

With Limestone.

Pull up a loop of Limestone in the BL in Rnd 15 at the center back of the cap.

Rnd 1: BL sc 20 sts in Rnd 15, BL sc 21 st in Rnd 18, BL sc 19 in Rnd 15. (60 sts)

Rnd 2: (Sc 8, sc2tog) x6. (54 sts)

Rnd 3: (Sc 7, sc2tog) x6. (48 sts)

Rnds 4–7: Sc in each st around.

Change to Lettuce.

Rnds 8–11: Sc in each st around.

Rnd 12: (Sc 7, sc 2 in next st) x6. (54 sts)

Rnds 13–16: Sc in each st around.

Place a locking marker in the loop while you make the face.

Position your gnome so that the visor of the cap is centered at the front, and the held st is at the center back.

Insert safety eyes between Rnds 3 and 4 of the head, 10 sts apart.

Embroider the cheeks with Dark Pink.

Rnd 17: (Sc 8, sc 2 in next st) x6. (60 sts)

Rnds 18–20: Sc in each st around.

Rnd 21: (FL sc 9, FL sc 2 in next st) x6. (66 sts)

Rnd 22: Sc in each st around.

Rnd 23: (Sc 10 sc 2 in next st) x6. (72 sts)

Rnd 24: Sc in each st around.

Fasten off and weave in the yarn ends.

Bottom

Pull up a loop of Limestone in the BL of any st of Rnd 20 of the robe.

Rnd 1: (BL sc 8 st, BL sc2tog) x6. (54 sts)

Rnd 2: (Sc 7, sc2tog) x6. (48 sts)

Rnd 3: (Sc 4, sc2tog) x8. (40 sts)

Rnd 4: (Sc 3, sc2tog) x8. (32 sts)

Rnd 5: (Sc 2, sc2tog) x8. (24 sts)

Stuff the body.

Rnd 6: (Sc 1, sc2tog) x8. (16 sts)

Rnd 7: (Sc2tog) x8. (8 sts)

Fasten off, leaving a long tail. Using a darning needle, weave the yarn tail through the FL of each st of the last rnd. Pull tight to close. Weave in the yarn end.

Arms (make 2)

With Limestone.

Rnd 1: Sc 6 into a MR. (6 sts)

Rnd 2: Sc 2 in each st around. (12 sts)

Rnds 3–4: Sc in each st around.

Change to Lettuce.

Rnds 5–12: Sc in each st around.

Lightly stuff the arm. Flatten the opening of the arm and work the next row through both layers to close.

Next Row: Sc 5 through both layers, sl st in the last st.

Fasten off, leaving a long tail for sewing.

Nose

With Limestone.

Rnd 1: Sc 6 into a MR. (6 sts)

Rnd 2: Sc 2 in each st around. (12 sts)

Rnd 3: (Sc 1, sc 2 in next st) x6. (18 sts)

Rnd 4: Sc in each st around.

Rnd 5: (Sc 1, sc2tog) x6. (12 sts)

Fasten off, leaving a long tail for sewing.

Feet (make 2)

With Teak.

Rnd 1: Sc 6 into a MR. (6 sts)

Rnd 2: Sc 2 in each st around. (12 sts)

Rnds 3–4: Sc in each st around.

The feet don't need to be stuffed. Flatten the opening of the foot and work the next row through both layers to close.

Next Row: Sc 5 through both layers, sl st in the last st.

Fasten off, leaving a long tail for sewing.

Beard

With White.

Rnd 1: Sc 6 into a MR. (6 sts)

Rnd 2: Sc in each st around.

Rnd 3: (Sc 1, sc 2 in next st) x3. (9 sts)

Rnd 4: Hdc 2 in next st, sc 8. (10 sts)

Rnd 5: Hdc 2 in next st, hdc 1, sc 2, hdc 1, hdc 2 in next st, hdc 1, sc 2, hdc 1. (12 sts)

Rnd 6: (Sc 1, sc 2 in next st) x6. (18 sts)

Rnd 7: (Sc 2 in next st, sc 8) x2. (20 sts)

Rnd 8: (Sc 3, sc 2 in next st) x5. (25 sts)

Rnd 9: Sc in each st around.

Rnd 10: (Sc 4, sc 2 in next st) x5. (30 sts)

Rnd 11: (Sc 2 in next st, sc 14) x2. (32 sts)

The beard doesn't need to be stuffed. Flatten the opening of the beard and work the next row through both layers to close.

Next Row: Sc 15 through both layers, sl st in the last st.

Fasten off, leaving a long tail for sewing.

Golf Bag

With Brunet.

Rnd 1: Sc 6 into a MR. (6 sts)

Rnd 2: Sc 2 in each st around. (12 sts)

Rnd 3: (Sc 1, sc 2 in next st) x6. (18 sts)

Rnd 4: (Sc 2, sc 2 in next st) x6. (24 sts)

Rnd 5: BL sc in each st around.

Rnds 6–18: Sc in each st around.

Row 1: Sc 3, sl st in next st, ch 1, turn. (3 sts)

Rows 2–16: Sc 3, ch 1, turn.

Row 17: Sc 3.

Fasten off, leaving a long tail for sewing.

Sew Row 17 to Rnd 7 of the golf bag to form the handle.

Golf Club Head (make 3)

With Black.

Ch 5.

Rnd 1: Sc in 2nd ch from hook, sc in next 3 ch, continue along the other side of the foundation ch, sc 4. (8 sts)

Rnds 2–3: Sc in each st around.

Rnd 4: (Sc 1, sc 2 in next st) x4. (12 sts)

Rnd 5: Sc in each st around.

Rnd 6: (Sc2tog) x6. (6 sts)

Fasten off, leaving a long tail. Using a darning needle, weave the yarn tail through the FL of each st of the last rnd. Pull tight to close. Weave in the yarn end.

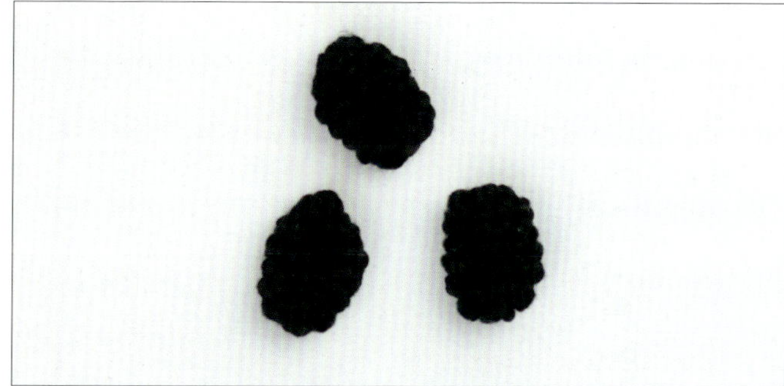

To make the shaft, cut 2.75in/7cm from the pointed end of a skewer stick. Color it with the permanent marker. Put a drop of glue on the pointed end of the shaft and insert it into the club head.

Time to Put It All Together!

Sew the beard, centered between the eyes and between Rnds 5 and 7 of the head.

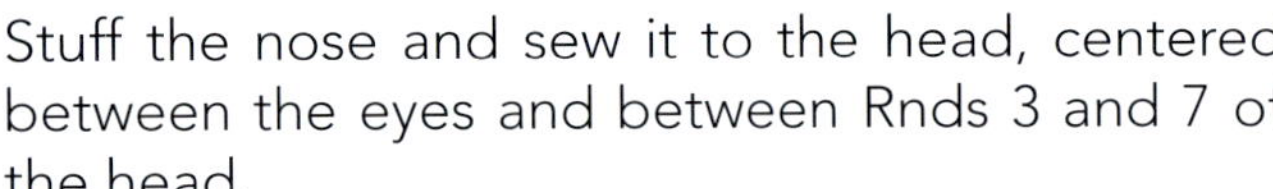

Stuff the nose and sew it to the head, centered between the eyes and between Rnds 3 and 7 of the head.

Sew the arms to the sides of the robe on Rnd 8 of the body, with 22 sts between them at the back.

Sew the feet to Rnd 1 at the bottom of the body, with 6 sts between them at the front.

HIKING GNOME

MATERIALS

Yarn

Yarn & Colors® 100% Mercerized Cotton (sport weight yarn) 1.75oz (50g)/137yds (125m)

Colors

Glass: 1.06oz (30g)/82yds (75m)

Rose Quartz: 0.35oz (10g)/27.3yds (25m)

Jade Gravel: 0.71oz (20g)/ 54.7yds (50m)

Dark Pink: leftovers

Brunet: leftover

Olive: leftovers

White: leftover

Teak: leftovers

Black: leftovers

- Size US 0 (2mm)) crochet hook (you may need to go up/down based on your tension)
- Size US 0000 (1.25mm) crochet hook
- Fiberfill
- 6mm black safety eyes
- Darning needle
- Locking stitch marker
- Scissors
- Pins
- 2 Skewer sticks
- Black permanent marker
- Pompom maker 1.5in/4cm diameter

Gauge

7 stitches x 7 rounds in 1in/2.54cm

Let's Begin!

Hat

With US 0 (2mm) crochet hook and Glass.

Rnd 1: Sc 6 into a MR. (6 sts)

Rnd 2: Sc 2 in each st around. (12 sts)

Rnd 3: (Sc 1, sc 2 in next st) x6. (18 sts)

Rnd 4: (Sc 2, sc 2 in next st) x6. (24 sts)

Rnd 5: (Sc 3, sc 2 in next st) x6. (30 sts)

Rnd 6: (Sc 4, sc 2 in next st) x6. (36 sts)

Rnd 7: (Sc 5, sc 2 in next st) x6. (42 sts)

Rnd 8: (Sc 6, sc 2 in next st) x6. (48 sts)

Rnd 9: (Sc 7, sc 2 in next st) x6. (54 sts)

Rnds 10–13: Sc in each st around.

Rnd 14: (Sc 8, sc 2 in next st) x6. (60 sts)

Rnds 15–18: Sc in each st around.

Change to Jade Gravel.

Rnd 19: (FL hdc 9, FL hdc 2 in next st) x6, sl st in first st to join. (66 sts)

Rnds 20–22: Ch 2, (front post hdc, back post hdc) x33, sl st in first st to join.

Fasten off and weave in the yarn ends.

Head and Robe

With Rose Quartz.

Pull up a loop of Rose Quartz in any BL of Rnd 18 of the hat.

Rnd 1: BL sc in each st around. (60 sts)

Rnd 2: (Sc 8, sc2tog) x6. (54 sts)

Rnd 3: (Sc 7, sc2tog) x6. (48 sts)

Rnds 4–7: Sc in each st around.

Change to Glass.

Rnds 8–11: Sc in each st around.

Rnd 12: (Sc 7, sc 2 in next st) x6. (54 sts)

Rnds 13–16: Sc in each st around.

Place a locking marker in the loop while you make the face.

Position your gnome so that the held loop is centered at the back.

Insert safety eyes between Rnds 3 and 4 of the head, 10 sts apart.

Embroider the cheeks with Dark Pink.

Rnd 17: (Sc 8, sc2 in next st) x6. (60 sts)

Rnds 18–20: Sc in each st around.

Rnd 21: (FL sc 9, FL sc 2 in next st) x6. (66 sts)

Rnd 22: Sc in each st around.

Rnd 23: (Sc 10, sc 2 in next st) x6. (72 sts)

Rnd 24: Sc in each st around.

Fasten off and weave in the yarn ends.

Bottom

Pull up a loop of Rose Quartz in the BL of any st of Rnd 20 of the robe.

Rnd 1: (BL sc 8, BL sc2tog) x6. (54 sts)

Rnd 2: (Sc 7, sc2tog) x6. (48 sts)

Rnd 3: (Sc 4, sc2tog) x8. (40 sts)

Rnd 4: (Sc 3, sc2tog) x8. (32 sts)

Rnd 5: (Sc 2, sc2tog) x8. (24 sts)

Stuff the body.

Rnd 6: (Sc 1, sc2tog) x8. (16 sts)

Rnd 7: (Sc2tog) x8. (8 sts)

Fasten off, leaving a long tail. Using a darning needle, weave the yarn tail through the FL of each st of the last rnd. Pull tight to close. Weave in the yarn end.

Make a 1.5in/4cm pompom with Jade Gravel and sew it to the top of the hat.

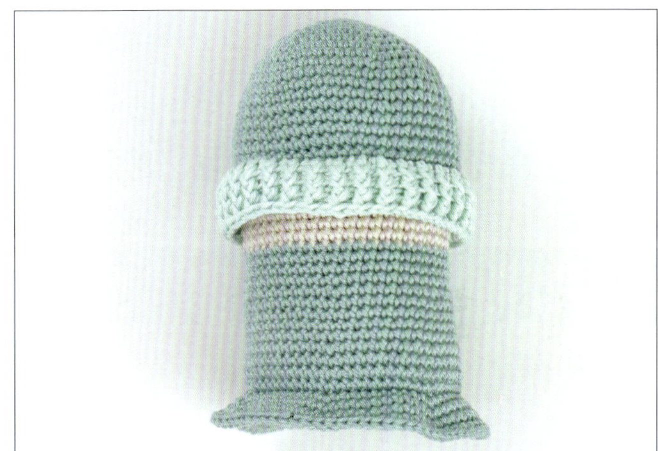

Arms (make 2)

With Rose Quartz.

Rnd 1: Sc 6 into a MR. (6 sts)

Rnd 2: Sc 2 in each st around. (12 sts)

Rnds 3–4: Sc in each st around.

Change to Glass.

Rnds 5–12: Sc in each st around.

Lightly stuff the arm. Flatten the opening of the arm and work the next row through both layers to close.

Next Row: Sc 5 through both layers, sl st in the last st.

Fasten off, leaving a long tail for sewing.

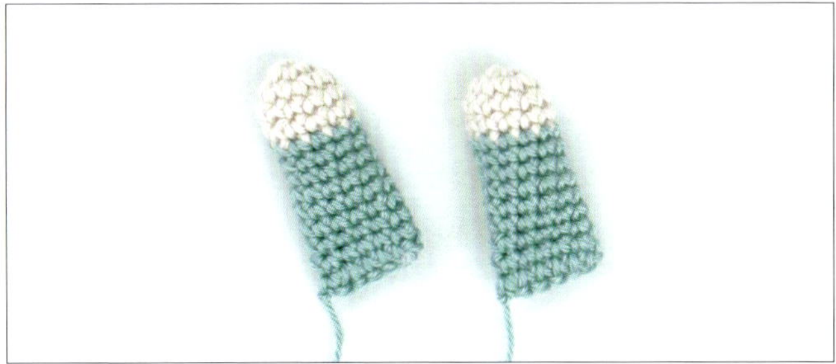

Nose

With Rose Quartz.

Rnd 1: Sc 6 into a MR. (6 sts)

Rnd 2: Sc 2 in each st around. (12 sts)

Rnd 3: (Sc 1, sc 2 in next st) x6. (18 sts)

Rnd 4: Sc in each st around.

Rnd 5: (Sc 1, sc2tog) x6. (12 sts)

Fasten off, leaving a long tail for sewing.

Feet (make 2)

With Teak.

Rnd 1: Sc 6 into a MR. (6 sts)

Rnd 2: Sc 2 in each st around. (12 sts)

Rnds 3–4: Sc in each st around.

The feet don't need to be stuffed. Flatten the opening of the foot and work the next row through both layers to close.

Next Row: Sc 5 through both layers, sl st in the last st.

Fasten off, leaving a long tail for sewing.

Mustaches (make 2)

With White.

Ch 7.

Rnd 1: Sl st in 2nd ch from the hook, sc 2 in next ch, hdc in next ch, dc in next ch, hdc in next ch, sc in next ch.

Fasten off, leaving a long tail for sewing.

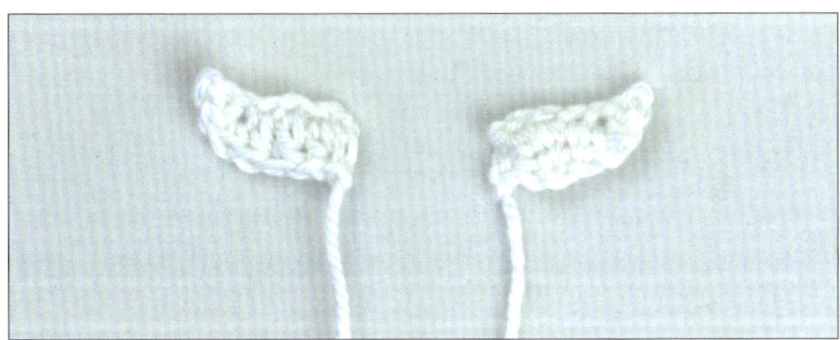

Backpack

With Olive.

Ch 16.

Rnd 1: Sc in 2nd ch from hook, sc in next 14 ch, continue along other side of foundation ch, sc in next 15 ch. (30 sts)

Rnds 2–13: Sc in each st around.

Row 14: Sc 2 to reach the edge of the backpack, ch 1, sc 14, ch 1, turn. (14 sts)

Rows 15–23: Sc 14, ch 1, turn.

Row 24: Sc in each st across.

Fasten off, leaving a long tail for sewing. Stuff the backpack lightly, fold the flap over the backpack and secure with a few sts.

Shoulder Straps (make 2)

With Brunet.

Ch 3.

Row 1: Sc in the 2nd ch from the hook, sc 1, ch 1, turn. (2 sts)

Rows 2–34: Sc 2, ch 1, turn.

Row 35: Sc 2.

Fasten off, leaving a long tail for sewing. Sew the straps to the backpack. With Black, embroider the "buckles."

Hiking Poles (make 2)

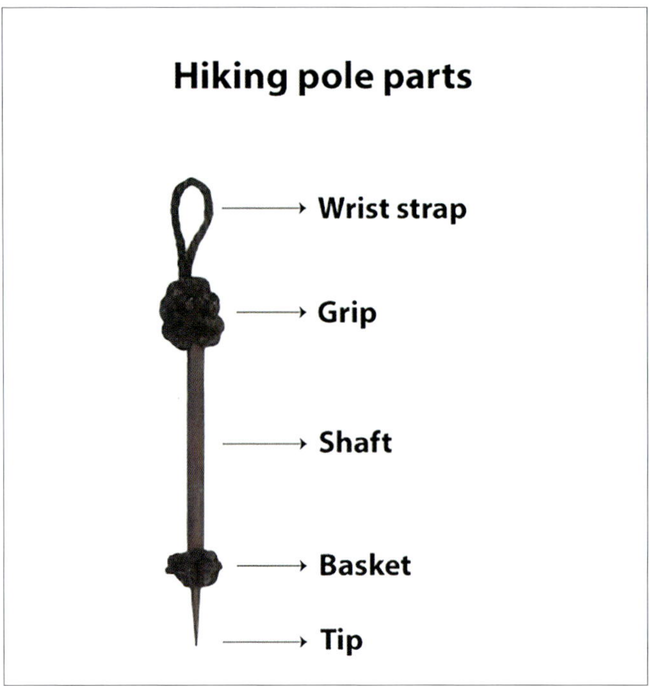

Cut 2in/5cm from the pointed end of a skewer stick. Color it with the permanent marker.

Grips (make 2)

With US 0000 (1.25mm) crochet hook and Black.

Rnd 1: Sc 6 into a MR. (6 sts)

Rnds 2–3: Sc in each st around.

Fasten off and weave in the yarn end.

Baskets (make 2)

With US 0000 (1.25mm) crochet hook and Black.

Rnd 1: Sc 6 into a MR. (6 sts)

Fasten off and weave in the yarn end.

Wrist Straps (make 2)

Cut a piece of Black yarn, fold it in half, and tie the ends together to form a loop. Insert the crochet hook through the center of Rnd 1 of the grip and pull the loop through to form the wrist strap.

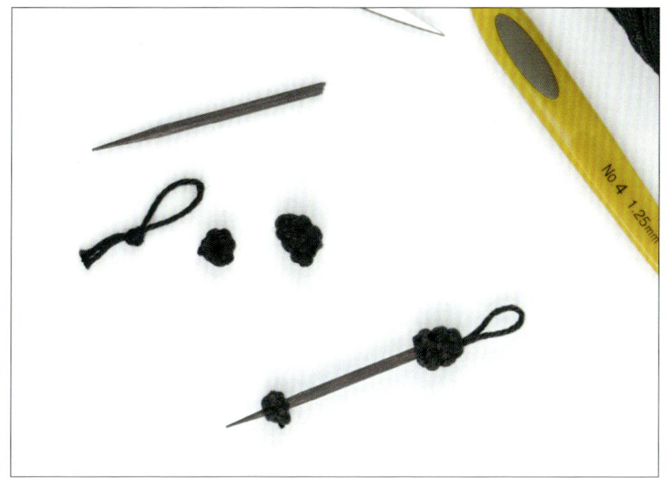

Assembly

Put a drop of glue on the blunt end of the shaft and insert it into the grip. Put a drop of glue in the basket and insert the tip of the shaft into the center of it. Make the other hiking pole in the same way.

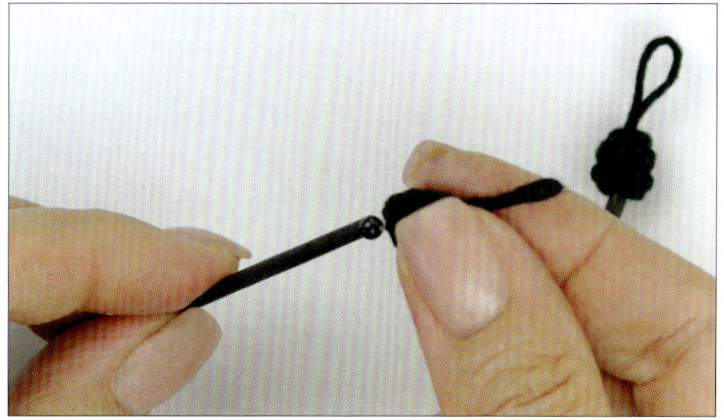

Time to Put It All Together!

Sew the mustaches, centered between the eyes and between Rnds 5 and 7 of the head, with 4 sts between them.

Stuff the nose and sew it to the head, centered between the mustaches and between Rnds 3 and 7 of the head.

Sew the arms to the sides of the robe on Rnd 8 of the body, with 22 sts between them at the back.

Sew the feet to Rnd 1 of the bottom, with 6 sts between them at the front.

Put the backpack on the back and the hiking poles in the hands.

KNITTING GNOME

MATERIALS

Yarn

Yarn & Colors® 100% Mercerized Cotton (sport weight yarn) 1.75oz (50g)/137yds (125m)

Colors

Clay: 0.35oz (10g)/27.3yds (25m)

Peridot: leftovers

Rose Quartz: 0.35oz (10g)/27.3yds (25m)

Lollipop: 0.71oz (20g) 54.7yds (50m)

Dark Pink: leftovers

Teak: leftovers

White: leftovers

Sunflower: leftover

Black: leftovers

Clematis: 0.35oz (10g)/27.3yds (25m)

- Size US 0 (2mm) crochet hook (you may need to go up/down based on your tension)
- US 0000 (1.25mm) crochet hook
- Fiberfill
- 6mm safety black safety eyes
- Darning needle
- Locking stitch marker
- Scissors
- Pins
- Skewer sticks
- Black permanent marker

Gauge

7 stitches x 7 rounds in 1in/2.54cm

Let's Begin!

Hat

With US 0 (2mm) crochet hook and Clay.

Rnd 1: Sc 6 into a MR. (6 sts)

Rnd 2: Sc 2 in each st around. (12 sts)

Rnd 3: (Sc 1, sc 2 in next st) x6. (18 sts)

Rnd 4: (Sc 2, sc 2 in next st) x6. (24 sts)

Rnd 5: (Sc 3, sc 2 in next st) x6. (30 sts)

Rnd 6: (Sc 4, sc 2 in next st) x6. (36 sts)

Rnd 7: (Sc 5, sc 2 in next st) x6. (42 sts)

Rnd 8: (Sc 6, sc 2 in next st) x6. (48 sts)

Rnd 9: (Sc 7, sc 2 in next st) x6. (54 sts)

Rnds 10–13: Sc in each st around.

Rnd 14: (Sc 8, sc 2 in next st) x6. (60 sts)

Rnd 15: Sc in each st around.

Change to Peridot.

Rnd 16: FL sc in each st around.

Rnds 17–18: Sc in each st around.

Change to Clay.

Rnd 19: (FL sc 9, FL sc 2 in next st) x6. (66 sts)

Rnd 20: (Sc 10, sc 2 in next st) x6. (72 sts)

Rnd 21: Sc 6, sc 2 in next st (sc 11, sc 2 in next st) x5, sc 5. (78 sts)

Rnd 22: (Sc 12, sc 2 in next st) x6. (84 sts)

Rnd 23: Sc in each st around.

Fasten off and weave in the yarn ends.

Head and Robe

With Rose Quartz.

Pull up a loop of Rose Quartz in any BL of Rnd 15 of the hat.

Rnd 1: BL sc in next 17 sts of Rnd 15, BL sc in next 26 sts of Rnd 18, then BL sc in next 17 sts of Rnd 15. (60 sts)

Rnd 2: (Sc 8, sc2tog) x6. (54 sts)

Rnd 3: (Sc 7, sc2tog) x6. (48 sts)

Rnds 4–7: Sc in each st around.

Change to Lollipop.

Rnds 8–11: Sc in each st around.

Rnd 12: (Sc 7, sc 2 in next st) x6. (54 sts)

Rnds 13–16: Sc in each st around.

Place a locking marker in the loop while you make the face.

Position your gnome so that the held loop is centered at the back.

Insert safety eyes between Rnds 3 and 4 of the head, 10 sts apart.

Embroider the cheeks with Dark Pink.

Rnd 17: (Sc 8, sc 2 in next st) x6. (60 sts)

Rnds 18–20: Sc in each st around.

Rnd 21: (FL sc 9, FL sc 2 in next st) x6. (66 sts)

Rnd 22: Sc in each st around.

Rnd 23: (Sc 10, sc 2 in next st) x6. (72 sts)

Rnd 24: Sc in each st around.

Fasten off and weave in the yarn ends.

Bottom

Pull up a loop of Rose Quartz in the BL of any st of Rnd 20 of the robe.

Rnd 1: (BL sc 8, BL sc2tog) x6. (54 sts)

Rnd 2: (Sc 7, sc2tog) x6. (48 sts)

Rnd 3: (Sc 4, sc2tog) x8. (40 sts)

Rnd 4: (Sc 3, sc2tog) x8. (32 sts)

Rnd 5: (Sc 2, sc2tog) x8. (24 sts)

Stuff the body.

Rnd 6: (Sc 1, sc2tog) x8. (16 sts)

Rnd 7: (Sc2tog) x8. (8 sts)

Fasten off, leaving a long tail. Using a darning needle, weave the yarn tail through the FL of each st of the last rnd. Pull tight to close. Weave in the yarn end.

Arms (make 2)

With Rose Quartz.

Rnd 1: Sc 6 into a MR. (6 sts)

Rnd 2: Sc 2 in each st around. (12 sts)

Rnds 3–4: Sc in each st around.

Change Lollipop.

Rnds 5–12: Sc in each st around.

Lightly stuff the arm. Flatten the opening of the arm and work the next row through both layers to close.

Next Row: Sc 5 through both layers, sl st in last st.

Fasten off, leaving a long tail for sewing.

Nose

With Rose Quartz.

Rnd 1: Sc 6 into a MR. (6 sts)

Rnd 2: Sc 2 in each st around. (12 sts)

Rnd 3: (Sc 1, sc 2 in next st) x6. (18 sts)

Rnd 4: Sc in each st around.

Rnd 5: (Sc 1, sc2tog) x6. (12 sts)

Fasten off, leaving a long tail for sewing.

Feet (make 2)

With Teak.

Rnd 1: Sc 6 into a MR. (6 sts)

Rnd 2: Sc 2 in each st around. (12 sts)

Rnds 3–4: Sc in each st around.

The feet don't need to be stuffed. Flatten the opening of the foot and work the next row through both layers to close.

Next Row: Sc 5 through both layers, sl st in last st.

Fasten off, leaving a long tail for sewing.

Beard

With White.

Start by making 5 parts for the beard, which will be joined together after all are made.

Rnd 1: Sc 5 into a MR. (5 sts)

Rnd 2: Sc 2 in each st around. (10 sts)

Fasten off the first 4 parts. Do not fasten off the fifth part. Continue by joining all the parts.

Rnd 3: Sc 5 along one side of the first part, sc 5 along one side of the second part, sc 5 along one of the third part, sc 10 around the fourth part, sc 5 along the remaining side of the third part, sc 5 along the remaining side of the second part, sc 5 along the remaining side of the first part, sc 10 around the fifth part. (50 sts)

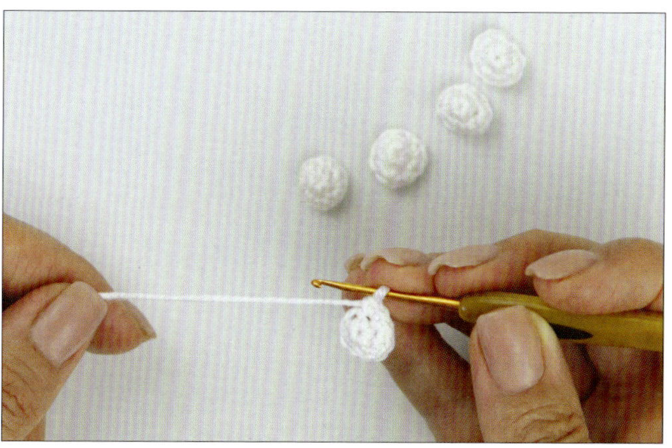

Rnd 4: Sc 4, sc2tog, (sc 3, sc2tog) x3, sc 8, sc2tog, (sc 3, sc2tog) x3, sc 4. (42 sts)

Rnd 5: Sc 3, sc2tog, (sc 2, sc2tog) x3, sc 7, sc2tog, (sc 2, sc2tog) x3, sc 4. (34 sts)

Rnd 6: (Sc 1, sc2tog) x5, (sc2tog) x2, (sc 1, sc2tog) x5. (22 sts)

Rnd 7: Sc 2, (sc2tog) x3, sc 5, (sc2tog) x3, sc 3. (16 sts)

Rnd 8: (Sc2tog) x8. (8 sts)

The beard doesn't need to be stuffed. Fasten off, leaving a long tail for sewing.

Flowers (make 3)

With White.

Rnd 1: Work (ch 3, dc, ch 3, sl st) x5 into a MR. Pull the tail to tighten the ring. (5 petals)

Fasten off, leaving a long tail for sewing.

Using Sunflower, make a French knot to form the center of the flower.

Knitting Needles (make 2)

Cut 2in/5cm from the pointed tip of 2 skewer sticks. Color each with the permanent marker.

Ends (make 2)

With a US 0000 (1.25mm) crochet hook and Black.

Rnd 1: Sc 6 into a MR. (6 sts)

Rnds 2–3: Sc in each st around.

Fasten off and weave in the yarn end. Put a drop of glue on the blunt end of the shaft and insert it into the end.

Wind a small ball of Clematis and stick the needles into the ball of yarn.

Time to Put It All Together!

Sew the beard, centered between the eyes and between Rnds 5 and 7 of the head.

Stuff the nose and sew it to the head, centered between the eyes and between Rnds 3 and 7 of the head.

Sew the arms to the sides of the robe, on Rnd 8 of the body, with 22 sts between them at the back.

Sew the feet to Rnd 1 at the bottom of the body, with 6 sts between them at the front.

Sew the flowers on one side of the hat.

PAINTING GNOME

MATERIALS

Yarn

Yarn & Colors® 100% Mercerized Cotton (sport weight yarn) 1.75oz (50g)/137yds (125m)

Colors

White: 1.06oz (30g)/82yds (75m)
Clay: 0.35oz (10g)/27.3yds (25m)
Teak: leftovers
Dark Pink: leftovers
Mustard: 0.35oz (10g)/27.3yds (25m)
Sunflower: leftovers
Pacific Blue: leftovers
Cardinal: leftovers
Pesto: leftover
Orange: leftover
Limestone: leftovers
Soft Gray: leftovers
Cream: leftovers

- Size US 0 (2mm) crochet hook (you may need to go up/down based on your tension)
- Fiberfill
- 6mm black safety eyes
- Darning needle
- Locking stitch marker
- Scissors
- Pins

Gauge

7 stitches x 7 rounds in 1in/2.54cm

Let's Begin!

Hat

With White.

Rnd 1: Sc 6 into a MR. (6 sts)

Rnds 2–3: Sc in each st around.

Rnd 4: Sc 5, sc 2 in next st. (7 sts)

Rnd 5: Sc 6, sc 2 in next st. (8 sts)

Rnd 6: Sc 7, sc 2 in next st. (9 sts)

Rnd 7: Sc 8, sc 2 in next st. (10 sts)

Rnd 8: Sc 9, sc 2 in next st. (11 sts)

Rnd 9: Sc 10, sc 2 in next st. (12 sts)

Rnd 10: Sc in each st around.

Rnd 11: (Sc 2, sc 2 in next st) x4. (16 sts)

Rnd 12: Sc in each st around.

Rnd 13: (Sc 1, sc 2 in next st) x8. (24 sts)

Rnds 14–17: Sc in each st around.

Rnd 18: (Sc 2, sc 2 in next st) x8. (32 sts)

Rnds 19–20: Sc in each st around.

Rnd 21: (Sc 3, sc 2 in next st) x8. (40 sts)

Rnd 22: (Sc 9, sc 2 in next st) x4. (44 sts)

Rnd 23: (Sc 10, sc 2 in next st) x4. (48 sts)

Rnd 24: Sc in each st around.

Rnd 25: (Sc 7, sc 2 in next st) x6. (54 sts)

Rnd 26: Sc in each st around.

Rnd 27: (Sc 8, sc 2 in next st) x6. (60 sts)

Rnds 28–29: Sc in each st around.

Rnd 30: (FL sc 9, FL sc 2 in next st) x6. (66 sts)

Rnd 31: Sc in each st around.

Rnd 32: (Sc 10, sc 2 in next st) x6. (72 sts)

Rnd 33: Sc in each st around.

Fasten off and weave in the yarn ends.

Head and Robe

With Clay.

Pull up a loop of Clay in any BL of Rnd 29 of the hat.

Rnd 1: BL sc in each st around. (60 sts)

Rnd 2: (Sc 8, sc2tog) x6. (54 sts)

Rnd 3: (Sc 7, sc2tog) x6. (48 sts)

Rnds 4–7: Sc in each st around.

Change to White.

Rnds 8–11: Sc in each st around.

Rnd 12: (Sc 7, sc 2 in next st) x6. (54 sts)

Rnds 13–16: Sc in each st around.

Place a locking marker in the loop while you make the face.

Position your gnome so that the held loop is centered at the back.

Insert safety eyes between Rnds 3 and 4 of the head, 10 sts apart.

Embroider the cheeks with Dark Pink.

Rnd 17: (Sc 8, sc 2 in next st) x6. (60 sts)

Rnds 18–20: Sc in each st around.

Rnd 21: (FL sc 9, FL sc 2 in next st) x6. (66 sts)

Rnd 22: Sc in each st around.

Rnd 23: (Sc 10, sc 2 in next st) x6. (72 sts)

Rnd 24: Sc in each st around.

Fasten off and weave in the yarn ends.

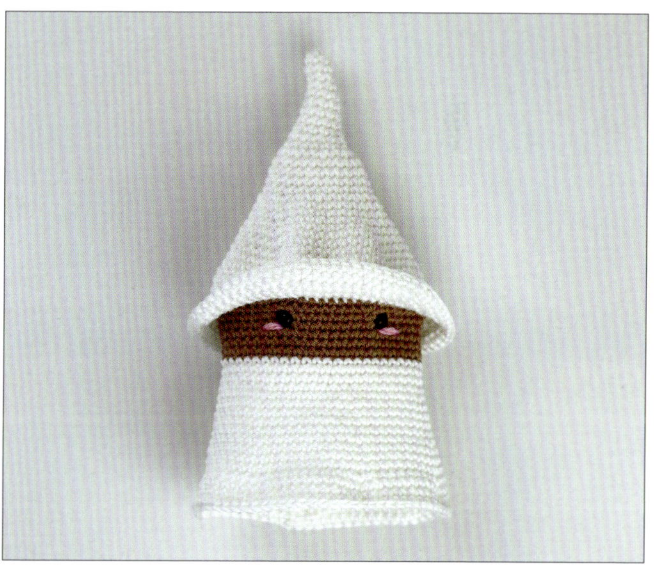

Paint Splotches (make 10)

Make two in Sunflower, two in Pacific Blue, two in Cardinal, two in Pesto and two in Orange.

Rnd 1: Sc 6 into a MR, sl st in first st to join. (6 sts)

Rnd 2: (Ch 6, sc in 2nd ch from hook, sc in next 4 ch, sc in next st of Rnd 1) x2, ch 4, sc in the 2nd ch from hook, sc in next 2 ch, sc in next 2 sts of Rnd 1, ch 5, sc in 2nd ch from hook, sc in next 3 ch, sc in next st of Rnd 1, ch 3, sc in 2nd ch from hook, sc in next ch, sc in next st of Rnd 1, sl st in Rnd 1 to join.

Fasten off and weave in the yarn ends. Sew the stains to the hat and robe wherever you like.

Bottom

Pull up a loop of Clay in the BL of any st of Rnd 20 of the robe.

Rnd 1: (BL sc 8, BL sc2tog) x6. (54 sts)

Rnd 2: (Sc 7, sc2tog) x6. (48 sts)

Rnd 3: (Sc 4, sc2tog) x8. (40 sts)

Rnd 4: (Sc 3, sc2tog) x8. (32 sts)

Rnd 5: (Sc 2, sc2tog) x8. (24 sts)

Stuff the body.

Rnd 6: (Sc 1, sc2tog) x8. (16 sts)

Rnd 7: (Sc2tog) x8. (8 sts)

Fasten off, leaving a long tail. Using a darning needle, weave the yarn tail through the FL of each st of the last rnd. Pull tight to close. Weave in the yarn end.

Arms (make 2)

With Clay.

Rnd 1: Sc 6 into a MR. (6 sts)

Rnd 2: Sc 2 in each st around. (12 sts)

Rnds 3–4: Sc in each st around.

Change to White.

Rnds 5–12: Sc in each st around.

Lightly stuff the arm. Flatten the opening of the arm and work the next row through both layers to close.

Next Row: Sc 5 through both layers, sl st in the last st.

Fasten off, leaving a long tail for sewing.

Nose

With Clay.

Rnd 1: Sc 6 into a MR. (6 sts)

Rnd 2: Sc 2 in each st around. (12 sts)

Rnd 3: (Sc 1, sc 2 in next st) x6. (18 sts)

Rnd 4: Sc in each st around.

Rnd 5: (Sc 1, sc2tog) x6. (12 sts)

Fasten off, leaving a long tail for sewing.

Feet (make 2)

With Teak.

Rnd 1: Sc 6 into a MR. (6 sts)

Rnd 2: Sc 2 in each st around. (12 sts)

Rnds 3–4: Sc in each st around.

The feet don't need to be stuffed. Flatten the opening of the foot and work the next row through both layers to close.

Next Row: Sc 5 through both layers, sl st in the last st.

Fasten off, leaving a long tail for sewing.

Beard

With Mustard.

Ch 23.

Row 1: Hdc 3 in 3rd ch from hook, (3 hdc in next ch) x11, sl st in next ch, (sl st in next ch, ch 14, hdc 3 in 3rd ch from hook, [hdc 3 in next ch] x11, sl st in next ch) x4.

Fasten off, leaving a long tail for sewing. Shape the 5 curls as needed.

Brush

With Limestone.

Rnd 1: Sc 6 into a MR. (6 sts)

Rnds 2–9: Sc in each st around.

Rnd 10: (Sc 2, sc 2 in next st) x2. (8 sts)

Rnds 11–24: Sc in each st around.

Change to Soft Gray.

Rnds 25–30: Sc in each st around.

Rnd 31: (Sc 2, sc2tog) x2. (6 sts)

Rnds 32–33: Sc in each st around.

Fasten off and weave in the yarn ends.

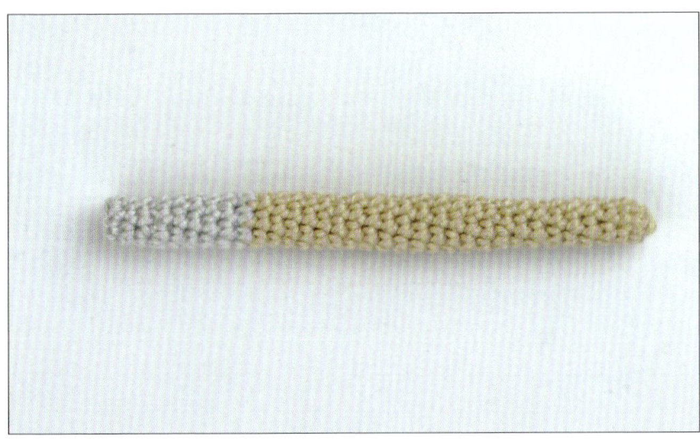

Pull up a loop of Cream in the BL of any st of Rnd 33.

Rnd 34: BL sc each st around. (6 sts)

Rnd 35: (Sc 1, sc 2 in next st) x3. (9 sts)

Rnd 36: (Sc 2, sc 2 in next st) x3. (12 sts)

Rnd 37: Sc in each st around.

Rnd 38: (Sc 2, sc2tog) x3. (9 sts)

Rnd 39: (Sc 1, sc2tog) x3. (6 sts)

Rnd 40: (Sc2tog) x3. (3 sts)

Fasten off and weave in the yarn ends.

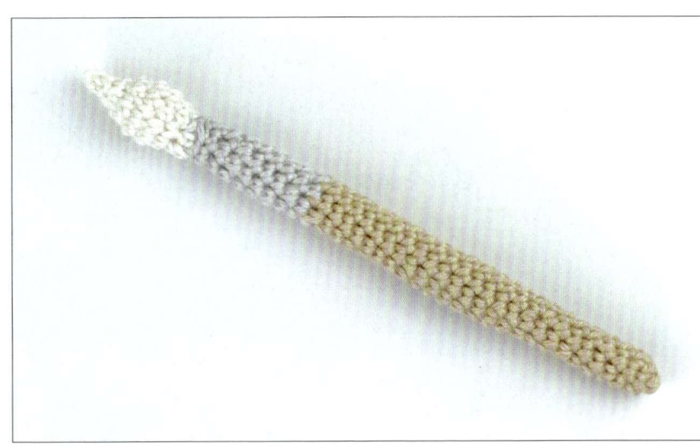

Time to Put It All Together!

Sew the beard, centered between the eyes and between Rnds 5 and 7 of the head.

Stuff the nose and sew it to the head, centered between the eyes and between Rnds 3 and 7 of the head.

Sew the arms to the sides of the robe on Rnd 8, with 22 sts between them at the back.

Sew the feet to Rnd 1 at the bottom of the body, with 6 sts between them at the front.

PHOTOGRAPHY GNOME

MATERIALS

Yarn

Yarn & Colors® 100% Mercerized Cotton (sport weight yarn) 1.75oz (50g)/137yds (125m)

Colors

Fawn: 1.06oz (30g)/82yds (75m)
Satay: leftovers
Limestone: 0.35oz (10g)/27.3yds (25m)
Dark Pink: leftovers
Teak: leftovers
White: leftovers
Black: leftovers
Ice Blue: leftovers

- Size US 0 (2mm) crochet hook (you may need to go up/down based on your tension)
- Fiberfill
- 6mm black safety eyes
- Darning needle
- Locking stitch marker
- Scissors
- Pins

Gauge

7 stitches x 7 rounds in 1in/2.54cm

Let's Begin!

Hat

With Fawn.

Rnd 1: Sc 6 into a MR. (6 sts)

Rnd 2: Sc 2 in each st around. (12 sts)

Rnd 3: (Sc 1, sc 2 in next st) x6. (18 sts)

Rnd 4: (Sc 2, sc 2 in next st) x6. (24 sts)

Rnd 5: (Sc 3, sc 2 in next st) x6. (30 sts)

Rnd 6: (Sc 4, sc 2 in next st) x6. (36 sts)

Rnd 7: (Sc 5, sc 2 in next st) x6. (42 sts)

Rnd 8: (Sc 6, sc 2 in next st) x6. (48 sts)

Rnd 9: (Sc 7, sc 2 in next st) x6. (54 sts)

Rnds 10–13: Sc in each st around.

Rnd 14: (Sc 8, sc 2 in next st) x6. (60 sts)

Rnd 15: Sc in each st around.

Change to Satay.

Rnd 16: FL sc in each st around.

Rnds 17–18: Sc in each st around.

Change to Fawn.

Rnd 19: (FL sc 9, FL sc 2 in next st) x6. (66 sts)

Rnd 20: (Sc 10, sc 2 in next st) x6. (72 sts)

Rnd 21: Sc 6, sc 2 in next st (sc 11, sc 2 in next st) x5, sc 5. (78 sts)

Rnd 22: (Sc 12, sc 2 in next st) x6. (84 sts)

Rnd 23: Sc in each st around.

Fasten off and weave in the yarn ends.

Head and Robe

With Limestone.

Pull up a loop of Limestone in any BL of Rnd 15 of the hat.

Rnd 1: BL sc in next 17 sts of Rnd 15, BL sc in next 26 sts of Rnd 18, then BL sc in next 17 sts of Rnd 15. (60 sts)

Rnd 2: (Sc 8, sc2tog) x6. (54 sts)

Rnd 3: (Sc 7, sc2tog) x6. (48 sts)

Rnds 4–7: Sc in each st around.

Change to Fawn.

Rnds 8–11: Sc in each st around.

Rnd 12: (Sc 7, sc 2 in next st) x6. (54 sts)

Rnd 13: Sc in each st around.

Change to Satay.

Rnds 14–16: Sc in each st around.

Place a locking marker in the loop while you make the face.

Position your gnome so that the held loop is centered at the back.

Insert safety eyes between Rnds 3 and 4 of the head, 10 sts apart.

Embroider the cheeks with Dark Pink.

Change to Fawn.

Rnd 17: (Sc 8, sc 2 in next st) x6. (60 sts)

Rnds 18–20: Sc in each st around.

Rnd 21: (FL sc 9, FL sc 2 in next st) x6. (66 sts)

Rnd 22: Sc in each st around.

Rnd 23: (Sc 10, sc 2 in next st) x6. (72 sts)

Rnd 24: Sc in each st around.

Fasten off and weave in the yarn ends. Make some sts at the center of the front with Black to simulate the belt buckle.

Bottom

Pull up a loop of Limestone in the BL of any st of Rnd 20 of the robe.

Rnd 1: (BL sc 8, BL sc2tog) x6. (54 sts)

Rnd 2: (Sc 7, sc2tog) x6. (48 sts)

Rnd 3: (Sc 4, sc2tog) x8. (40 sts)

Rnd 4: (Sc 3, sc2tog) x8. (32 sts)

Rnd 5: (Sc 2, sc2tog) x8. (24 sts)

Stuff the body.

Rnd 6: (Sc 1, sc2tog) x8. (16 sts)

Rnd 7: (Sc2tog) x8. (8 sts)

Fasten off, leaving a long tail. Using a darning needle, weave the yarn tail through the FL of each st of the last rnd. Pull tight to close. Weave in the yarn end.

Arms (make 2)

With Limestone.

Rnd 1: Sc 6 into a MR. (6 sts)

Rnd 2: Sc 2 in each st around. (12 sts)

Rnds 3–4: Sc in each st around.

Change to Fawn.

Rnds 5–12: Sc in each st around.

Lightly stuff the arm. Flatten the opening of the arm and work the next row through both layers to close.

Next Row: Sc 5 through both layers, sl st in the last st.

Fasten off, leaving a long tail for sewing.

Nose

With Limestone.

Rnd 1: Sc 6 into a MR. (6 sts)

Rnd 2: Sc 2 in each st around. (12 sts)

Rnd 3: (Sc 1, sc 2 in next st) x6. (18 sts)

Rnd 4: Sc in each st around.

Rnd 5: (Sc 1, sc2tog) x6. (12 sts)

Fasten off, leaving a long tail for sewing.

Feet (make 2)

With Teak.

Rnd 1: Sc 6 into a MR. (6 sts)

Rnd 2: Sc 2 in each st around. (12 sts)

Rnds 3–4: Sc in each st around.

The feet don't need to be stuffed. Flatten the opening of the foot and work the next row through both layers to close.

Next Row: Sc 5 through both layers, sl st in the last st.

Fasten off, leaving a long tail for sewing.

Mustaches (make 2)

With White.

Ch 7.

Rnd 1: Sl st in 2nd ch from hook, sc 2 in next ch, hdc in next ch, dc in next ch, hdc in next ch, sc in next ch. (7 sts)

Fasten off, leaving a long tail for sewing.

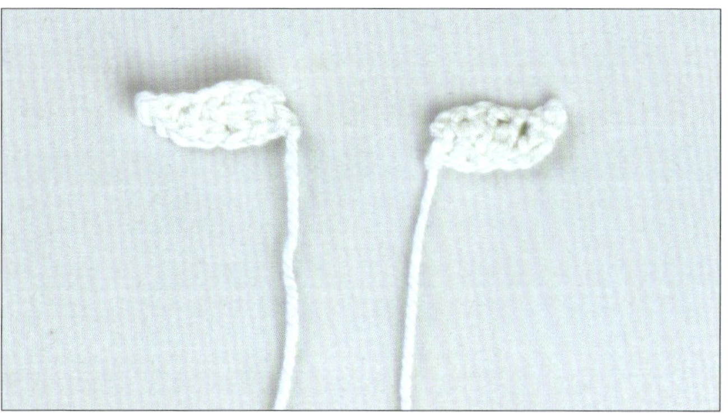

Camera Lens

With Ice Blue.

Rnd 1: Sc 6 into a MR, sl st in first st to join. (6 sts)

Rnd 2: Ch 1, sc in each st around, sl st in first st to join.

Fasten off, leaving a long tail for sewing.

Camera

Ch 11.

Row 1: Sc in 2nd ch from hook, sc in next 9 ch, ch 1, turn. (10 sts)

Rows 2–5: Sc in each st across, ch 1, turn.

Row 6: BL sc in each st across, ch 1, turn.

Rows 7–9: Sc in each st across, ch 1, turn.

Row 10: Sc in each st across.

Fasten off, leaving a long tail for sewing.

Sew the lens to the camera between Rows 2 and 4. Use Ice Blue to make a few sts next to the lens between Rows 4 and 5 to simulate the flash. Fold the camera in half and sew the edges together. Make a neck strap 50 ch long and sew an end to each side of the camera.

Time to Put It All Together!

Sew the mustaches centered between the eyes and between Rnds 5 and 7 of the head, with 4 sts between them.)

Stuff the nose and sew it, centered between the eyes and between Rnds 3 and 7 of the head.

Sew the arms to the sides of the robe, at Rnd 8, with 22 sts between them at the back.

Sew the feet to Rnd 1 at the bottom of the body, with 6 sts between them at the front.

Place the camera over the head and around the neck.

READING GNOME

MATERIALS

Yarn

Yarn & Colors® 100% Mercerized Cotton (sport weight yarn) 1.75oz (50g)/137yds (125m)

Colors

Pink Blossom: 1.06oz (30g)/82yds (75m)
Clay: 0.35oz (10g)/27.3yds (25m)
Jade Gravel: 1.06oz (30g)/82yds (75m)
Dark Pink: leftovers
White: 1.06oz (30g)/82yds (75m)
Teak: leftovers
Lettuce: leftovers
Cardinal: leftovers
Sunflower: leftovers
Navy Blue: leftovers

- Size US 0 (2mm) crochet hook (you may need to go up/down based on your tension)
- Fiberfill
- 6mm black safety eyes
- Darning needle
- Locking stitch marker
- Scissors
- Pins

Gauge

7 stitches x 7 rounds in 1in/2.54cm

Let's Begin!

Hat

With Blossom.

Rnd 1: Sc 6 into a MR. (6 sts)

Rnds 2–3: Sc in each st around.

Rnd 4: Sc 5, sc 2 in next st. (7 sts)

Rnd 5: Sc 6, sc 2 in next st. (8 sts)

Rnd 6: Sc 7, sc 2 in next st. (9 sts)

Rnd 7: Sc 8, sc 2 in next st. (10 sts)

Rnd 8: Sc 9, sc 2 in next st. (11 sts)

Rnd 9: Sc 10, sc 2 in next st. (12 sts)

Rnd 10: Sc in each st around.

Rnd 11: (Sc 2, sc 2 in next st) x4. (16 sts)

Rnd 12: Sc in each st around.

Rnd 13: (Sc 1, sc 2 in next st) x8. (24 sts)

Rnds 14–17: Sc in each st around.

Rnd 18: (Sc 2, sc 2 in next st) x8. (32 sts)

Rnds 19–20: Sc in each st around.

Rnd 21: (Sc 3, sc 2 in next st) x8. (40 sts)

Rnd 22: (Sc 9, sc 2 in next st) x4. (44 sts)

Rnd 23: (Sc 10, sc 2 in next st) x4. (48 sts)

Rnd 24: Sc in each st around.

Rnd 25: (Sc 7, sc 2 in next st) x6. (54 sts)

Rnd 26: Sc in each st around.

Rnd 27: (Sc 8, sc 2 in next st) x6. (60 sts)

Rnds 28–29: Sc in each st around.

Rnd 30: (FL hdc 9, FL hdc 2 in next st) x6, sl st in top of first st to join. (66 sts)

Rnds 31–33: Ch 2, (front post hdc, back post hdc) x33, sl st in top of first st to join.

Fasten off and weave in the yarn ends.

Head and Robe

With Clay.

Pull up a loop of Clay in the BL in the last st of Rnd 29 of the hat.

Rnd 1: BL sc in each st around. (60 sts)

Rnd 2: (Sc 8, sc2tog) x6. (54 sts)

Rnd 3: (Sc 7, sc2tog) x6. (48 sts)

Rnds 4–7: Sc in each st around.

Change to Jade Gravel.

Rnds 8–11: Sc in each st around.

Rnd 12: (Sc 7, sc 2 in next st) x6. (54 sts)

Rnds 13–16: Sc in each st around.

Place a locking marker in the loop while you make the face.

Position your gnome so that the held loop is centered at the back.

Insert safety eyes between Rnds 3 and 4 of the head, 10 sts apart.

Embroider the cheeks with Dark Pink.

Rnd 17: (Sc 8, sc 2 in next st) x6. (60 sts)

Rnds 18–20: Sc in each st around.

Rnd 21: (FL sc, FL sc 2 in next st) x6. (66 sts)

Rnd 22: Sc in each st around

Rnd 23: (Sc 10, sc 2 in next st) x6. (72 sts)

Rnd 24: Sc in each st around.

Fasten off and weave in the yarn ends.

Bottom

Pull up a loop of Clay in the BL of any st of Rnd 20 of the robe.

Rnd 1: (BL sc 8, BL sc2tog) x6. (54 sts)

Rnd 2: (Sc 7, sc2tog) x6. (48 sts)

Rnd 3: (Sc 4, sc2tog) x8. (40 sts)

Rnd 4: (Sc 3, sc2tog) x8. (32 sts)

Rnd 5: (Sc 2, sc2tog) x8. (24 sts)

Stuff the body.

Rnd 6: (Sc 1, sc2tog) x8. (16 sts)

Rnd 7: (Sc2tog) x8. (8 sts)

Fasten off, leaving a long tail. Using a darning needle, weave the yarn tail through the FL of each st of last rnd. Pull tight to close. Weave in the yarn end.

Arms (make 2)

With Clay.

Rnd 1: Sc 6 into a MR. (6 sts)

Rnd 2: Sc 2 in each st around. (12 sts)

Rnds 3–4: Sc in each st around.

Change to Jade Gravel.

Rnds 5–12: Sc in each st around.

Lightly stuff the arm. Flatten the opening of the arm and work the next row through both layers to close.

Next Row: Sc 5 through both layers, sl st in the last st.

Fasten off, leaving a long tail for sewing.

Nose

With Clay.

Rnd 1: Sc 6 into a MR. (6 sts)

Rnd 2: Sc 2 in each st around. (12 sts)

Rnd 3: (Sc 1, sc 2 in next st) x6. (18 sts)

Rnd 4: Sc in each st around.

Rnd 5: (Sc 1, sc2tog) x6. (12 sts)

Fasten off, leaving a long tail for sewing.

Feet (make 2)

With Teak.

Rnd 1: Sc 6 into a MR. (6 sts)

Rnd 2: Sc 2 in each st around. (12 sts)

Rnds 3–4: Sc in each st around.

The feet don't need to be stuffed. Flatten the opening of the foot and work the next row through both layers to close.

Next Row: Sc 5 through both layers, sl st in the last st.

Fasten off, leaving a long tail for sewing.

Braid Tips (make 2)

With White.

Rnd 1: Leaving a long tail, sc 6 into a MR. (6 sts)

Rnd 2: Sc 2 in each st around. (12 sts)

Rnds 3–4: Sc in each st around.

The tip doesn't need to be stuffed.

Rnd 5: (Sc2tog) x6. (6 sts)

Rnd 6: (Sc2tog) x3. (3 sts)

Fasten off, leaving a long tail for sewing.

Braids (make 2)

With White.

Ch 18.

Row 1: Sc in 2nd ch from hook, sc in next 14 ch, sl st in next ch, ch 16, sc in 2nd ch from hook, sc in next 14 ch, sl st in next ch, ch 16, sc in 2nd ch from hook, sc in next 14 ch.

Fasten off, leaving a long tail for sewing. Holding the end down with a pin, braid the 3 strands

together. Sew the braid tip to this end. Twist a length of Blossom around the join a few times.

Book Covers (make 4)

One in Lettuce, one in Sunflower, one in Cardinal and one in Navy Blue

Ch 11.

Row 1: Sc in 2nd ch from hook, sc in next 9 ch, ch 1, turn. (10 sts)

Rows 2–9: Sc in each st across, ch 1, turn.

Row 10: BL sc in in each st across, ch 1, turn.

Row 11: Sc in each st across, ch 1, turn.

Row 12: BL sc in each st across, ch 1, turn.

Rows 13–18: Sc in each st across, ch 1, turn.

Row 19: Sc in each st across.

Fasten off, leaving a long tail for sewing.

Book Pages (make 4)

With White.

Ch 9.

Row 1: Sc in 2nd ch from hook, sc in next 7 ch, ch 1, turn. (8 sts)

Rows 2–13: Sc in each st across, ch 1, turn.

Row 14: Sc in each st across.

Fasten off, leaving a long tail for sewing. Fold the page in half and secure the 2 layers with a few sts. Fold the cover in half and place the pages inside the cover. Hold the 4 layers together with a few sts.

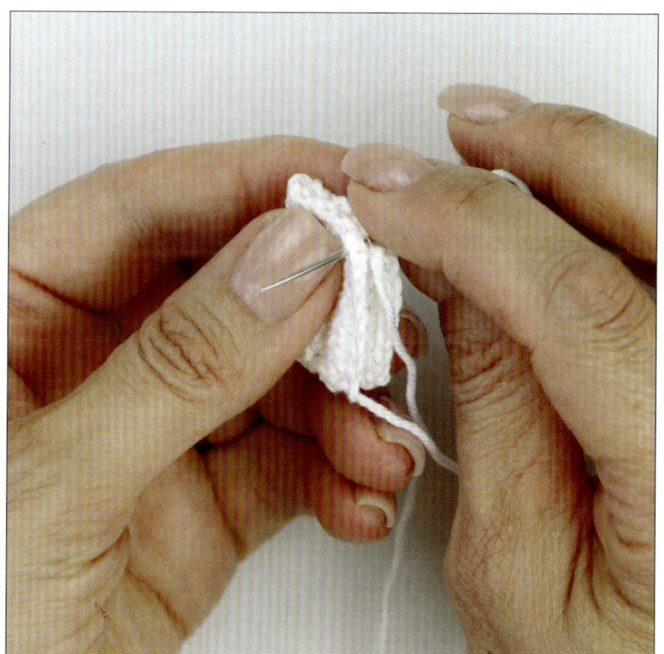

Time to Put It All Together!

Sew the braids at the sides of Rnd 1 of the head, with 19 sts between them at the front.

Stuff the nose and sew it, centered between the eyes and between Rnds 3 and 7 of the head.

Sew the arms to the sides of the robe, on Rnd 8, with 22 sts between them at the back.

Sew the feet to Rnd 1 at the bottom of the body, with 6 sts between them at the front.

RUNNING GNOME

MATERIALS

Yarn

Yarn & Colors® 100% Mercerized Cotton (sport weight yarn) 1.75oz (50g)/137yds (125m)

Colors

Pink Cardinal: 0.35oz (10g)/27.3yds (25m)
Limestone: 0.35oz (10g)/27.3yds (25m)
Sunflower: 0.71oz (20g)/54.7yds (50m)
Dark Pink: leftovers
Brunet: leftovers
Peony Leaf: leftovers
Teak: leftovers

- Size US 0 (2mm) crochet hook (you may need to go up/down based on your tension)
- Fiberfill
- 6mm black safety eyes
- Darning needle
- Locking stitch marker
- Scissors
- Pins

Gauge

7 stitches x 7 rounds in 1in/2.54cm

Let's Begin!

Cap

With Cardinal.

Rnd 1: Sc 6 in a MR. (6 sts)

Rnd 2: Sc 2 in each st around. (12 sts)

Rnd 3: (Sc 1, sc 2 in next st) x6. (18 sts)

Rnd 4: (Sc 2, sc 2 in next st) x6. (24 sts)

Rnd 5: (Sc 3, sc 2 in next st) x6. (30 sts)

Rnd 6: (Sc 4, sc 2 in next st) x6. (36 sts)

Rnd 7: (Sc 5, sc 2 in next st) x6. (42 sts)

Rnd 8: (Sc 6, sc 2 in next st) x6. (48 sts)

Rnd 9: (Sc 7, sc 2 in next st) x6. (54 sts)

Rnds 10–13: Sc in each st around.

Rnd 14: (Sc 8, sc 2 in next st) x6. (60 sts)

Rnd 15: Sc in each st around.

Rnd 16: FL sc in each st around.

Rnds 17–18: Sc in each st around.

Row 1: FL sc 21, ch 1, turn. (21 sts)

Row 2: Sc 4, (sc 2 in next st, sc) x4 times, sc 2 in next st, sc 4, ch 1, turn. (26 sts)

Row 3: Skip first st, sc in next 23 sts, skip next st, sc in next st, ch 1, turn. (24 sts)

Row 4: Skip first st, sc in next 21 sts, skip next st, sc in next st. (22 sts)

Fasten off and weave in the yarn ends.

Pull up a loop of Cardinal in the center st of Rnd 18 at the back of the cap. Work 1 rnd of sc along the entire edge of the cap. Fasten off and weave in the yarn ends.

Head and Robe

With Limestone.

Pull up a loop of Limestone in the BL in Rnd 15 at the center back of the cap.

Rnd 1: BL sc in next 20 sts of Rnd 15, BL sc in next 21 sts of Rnd 18, then BL sc in next 19 sts of Rnd 15. (60 sts)

Rnd 2: (Sc 8, sc2tog) x6. (54 sts)

Rnd 3: (Sc 7, sc2tog) x6. (48 sts)

Rnds 4–7: Sc in each st around.

Change to Sunflower.

Rnds 8–11: Sc in each st around.

Rnd 12: (Sc 7, sc 2 in next st) x6. (54 sts)

Rnds 13–16: Sc in each st around.

Place a locking marker in the loop while you make the face.

Position your gnome so that the held loop is centered at the back.

Insert safety eyes between Rnds 3 and 4 of the head, 10 sts apart.

Embroider the cheeks with Dark Pink.

Rnd 17: (Sc 8, sc 2 in next st) x6. (60 sts)

Rnds 18–20: Sc in each st around.

Rnd 21: (FL sc 9, FL sc 2 in next st) x6. (66 sts)

Rnd 22: Sc in each st around.

Rnd 23: (Sc 10, sc 2 in next st) x6. (72 sts)

Rnd 24: Sc in each st around.

Fasten off and weave in the yarn ends.

Bottom

Pull up a loop of Limestone in the BL of any st of Rnd 20 of the robe.

Rnd 1: (BL sc 8, BL sc2tog) x6. (54 sts)

Rnd 2: (Sc 7, sc2tog) x6. (48 sts)

Rnd 3: (Sc 4, sc2tog) x8. (40 sts)

Rnd 4: (Sc 3, sc2tog) x8. (32 sts)

Rnd 5: (Sc 2, sc2tog) x8. (24 sts)

Stuff the body.

Rnd 6: (Sc 1, sc2tog) x8. (16 sts)

Rnd 7: (Sc2tog) x8. (8 sts)

Fasten off, leaving a long tail. Using a darning needle, weave the yarn tail through the FL of each st of the last rnd. Pull tight to close. Weave in the yarn end.

Arms (make 2)

With Limestone.

Rnd 1: Sc 6 into a MR. (6 sts)

Rnd 2: Sc 2 in each st around. (12 sts)

Rnds 3–4: Sc in each st around.

Change to Sunflower.

Rnds 5–12: Sc in each st around.

Lightly stuff the arm. Flatten the opening of the arm and work the next row through both layers to close.

Next Row: Sc 5 through both layers, sl st in the last.

Fasten off, leaving a long tail for sewing.

Nose

With Limestone.

Rnd 1: Sc 6 into a MR. (6 sts)

Rnd 2: Sc 2 in each st around. (12 sts)

Rnd 3: (Sc 1, sc 2 in next st) x6. (18 sts)

Rnd 4: Sc in each st around.

Rnd 5: (Sc 1, sc2tog) x6. (12 sts)

Fasten off, leaving a long tail for sewing.

Feet (make 2)

With Teak.

Rnd 1: Sc 6 into a MR. (6 sts)

Rnd 2: Sc 2 in each st around. (12 sts)

Rnds 3–4: Sc in each st around.

The feet don't need to be stuffed. Flatten the opening of the foot and work the next row through both layers to close.

Next Row: Sc 5 through both layers, sl st in the last st.

Fasten off, leaving a long tail for sewing.

Beard

With Brunet.

Ch 23.

Row 1: Hdc 3 in 3rd ch from hook, (hdc 3 in next ch) x11, sl st in next ch, (sl st in next ch, ch 14, hdc 3 in 3rd ch from hook, (hdc 3 in next ch) x11, sl st in next ch) x4.

Fasten off, leaving a long tail for sewing. Shape the 5 curls as needed.

Headphones

With Peony Leaf.

Ear Pads (make 2)

Rnd 1: Sc 6 into a MR. (6 sts)

Rnd 2: Sc 2 in each st around. (12 sts)

Rnd 3: (Sc 1, sc 2 in next st) x6. (18 sts)

Rnds 4–6: Sc in each st around.

Fasten off, leaving a long tail for sewing.

Headband

Ch 39.

Row 1: Sl st in 2nd ch from hook, sl st in next 37 ch. (38 sts)

Fasten off, leaving a long tail for sewing.

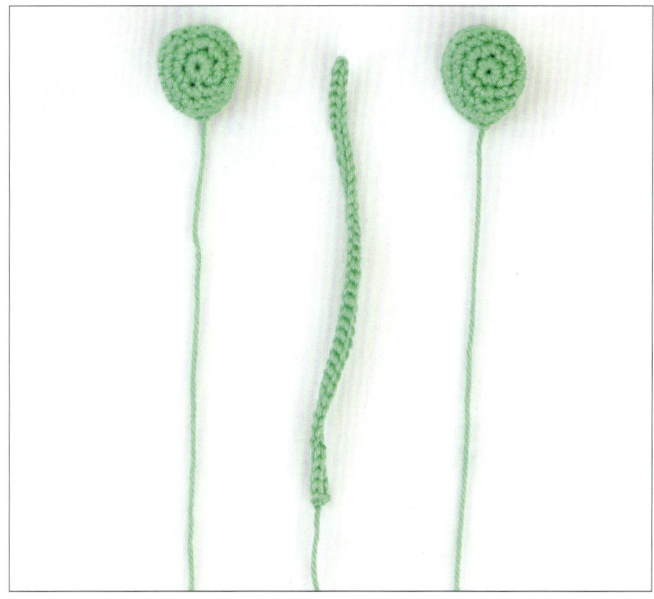

Time to Put It All Together!

Sew the beard, centered between the eyes and between Rnds 5 and 7 of the head.

Stuff the nose and sew it, centered between the eyes, between Rnds 3 and 7 of the head. Center the headband on the cap and sew then ends to the sides of the cap at Rnd 17.

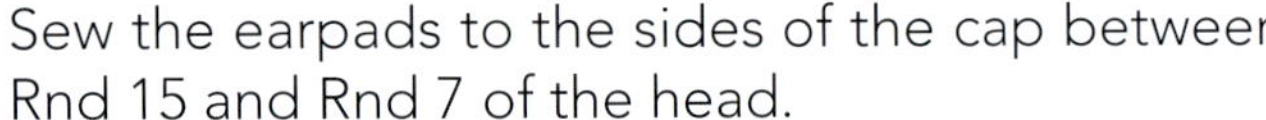

Sew the earpads to the sides of the cap between Rnd 15 and Rnd 7 of the head.

Sew the arms to the sides of the robe, on Rnd 8 with 22 sts between them at the back.

Sew the feet to Rnd 1 at the bottom of the body, with 6 sts between them at the front.

SAILING GNOME

MATERIALS

Yarn

Yarn & Colors® 100% Mercerized Cotton (sport weight yarn) 1.75oz (50g)/137yds (125m)

Colors

Brunet: 1.75oz (50g)/137yds (125m)
Navy Blue: 1.75oz (50g)/137yds (125m)
Cardinal: 0.35oz (10g)/27.3yds (25m)
Limestone: 0.35oz (10g)/27.3yds (25m)
Rose Quartz: leftovers
Dark Pink: leftovers
White: 0.35oz (10g)/27.3yds (25m)
Teak: leftovers

- Size US 0 (2mm) crochet hook (you may need to go up/down based on your tension)
- Fiberfill
- 6mm black safety eyes
- Darning needle
- Locking stitch marker
- Scissors
- Pins
- Cardboard or plastic to reinforce the base of the boat
- Skewer stick

Gauge

7 stitches x 7 rounds in 1in/2.54cm

Let's Begin!

Hat

With Navy Blue.

Rnd 1: Sc 6 into a MR. (6 sts)

Rnds 2–3: Sc in each st around.

Change to White.

Rnd 4: Sc 5, sc 2 in next st. (7 sts)

Rnd 5: Sc 6, sc 2 in next st. (8 sts)

Change to Navy Blue.

Rnd 6: Sc 7, sc 2 in next st. (9 sts)

Rnd 7: Sc 8, sc 2 in next st. (10 sts)

Change to White.

Rnd 8: Sc 9, sc 2 in next st. (11 sts)

Rnd 9: Sc 10, sc 2 in next st. (12 sts)

Change to Navy Blue.

Rnd 10: Sc in each st around.

Rnd 11: (Sc 2, sc 2 in next st) x4. (16 sts)

Change to White.

Rnd 12: Sc in each st around.

Rnd 13: (Sc 1, sc 2 in next st) x8. (24 sts)

Change to Navy Blue.

Rnds 14–15: Sc in each st around.

Change to White.

Rnds 16–17: Sc in each st around.

Change to Navy Blue.

Rnd 18: (Sc 2, sc 2 in next st) x8. (32 sts)

Rnd 19: Sc in each st around.

Change to White.

Rnd 20: Sc in each st around.

Rnd 21: (Sc 3, sc 2 in next st) x8. (40 sts)

Change to Navy Blue.

Rnd 22: (Sc 9, sc 2 in next st) x4. (44 sts)

Rnd 23: (Sc 10, sc 2 in next st) x4. (48 sts)

Rnd 24: Sc in each st around.

Change to White.

Rnd 25: (Sc 7, sc 2 in next st) x6. (54 sts)

Change to Navy Blue.

Rnd 26: Sc in each st around.

Rnd 27: (Sc 8, sc 2 in next st) x6. (60 sts)

Change to White.

Rnds 28–29: Sc in each st around.

Change to Navy Blue.

Rnd 30: (FL sc 9, FL sc 2 in next st) x6. (66 sts)

Rnd 31: Sc in each st around.

Change to White.

Rnd 32: (Sc 10, sc 2 in next st) x6. (72 sts)

Rnd 33: Sc in each st around.

Fasten off and weave in the yarn ends.

Head and Robe

With Rose Quartz.

Pull up a loop of Rose Quartz in the BL of the first st of Rnd 29.

Rnd 1: BL sc in each st around. (60 sts)

Rnd 2: (Sc 8, sc2tog) x6. (54 sts)

Rnd 3: (Sc 7, sc2tog) x6. (48 sts)

Rnds 4–7: Sc in each st around.

Change to Navy Blue.

Rnds 8–11: Sc in each st around.

Rnd 12: (Sc 7, sc 2 in next st) x6. (54 sts)

Rnds 13–16: Sc in each st around.

Place a locking marker in the loop while you make the face.

Position your gnome so that the held loop is centered at the back.

Insert safety eyes between Rnds 3 and 4 of the head, 10 sts apart.

Embroider the cheeks with Dark Pink.

Rnd 17: (Sc 8, sc 2 in next st) x6. (60 sts)

Rnds 18–20: Sc in each st around.

Rnd 21: (FL sc 9, FL sc 2 in next st) x6. (66 sts)

Rnd 22: Sc in each st around.

Rnd 23: (Sc 10, sc 2 in next st) x6. (72 sts)

Rnd 24: Sc in each st around.

Fasten off and weave in the yarn ends.

Bottom

Pull up a loop of Rose Quartz in the BL of any st of Rnd 20 of the robe.

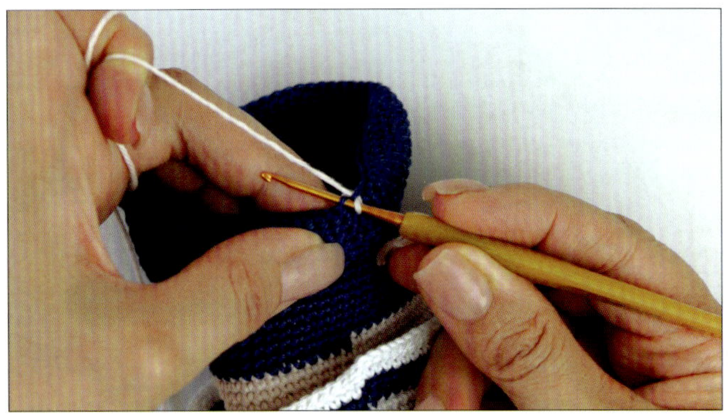

Rnd 1: (BL sc 8, BL sc2tog) x6. (54 sts)

Rnd 2: (Sc 7, sc2tog) x6. (48 sts)

Rnd 3: (Sc 4, sc2tog) x8. (40 sts)

Rnd 4: (Sc 3, sc2tog) x8. (32 sts)

Rnd 5: (Sc 2, sc2tog) x8. (24 sts)

Stuff the body.

Rnd 6: (Sc 1, sc2tog) x8. (16 sts)

Rnd 7: (Sc2tog) x8. (8 sts)

Fasten off, leaving a long tail. Using a darning needle, weave the yarn tail through the FL of each st of the last rnd. Pull tight to close. Weave in the yarn end.

Arms (make 2)

With Rose Quartz.

Rnd 1: Sc 6 into a MR. (6 sts)

Rnd 2: Sc 2 in each st around. (12 sts)

Rnds 3–4: Sc in each st around.

Change to Navy Blue.

Rnds 5–12: Sc in each st around.

Lightly stuff the arm. Flatten the opening of the arm and work the next row through both layers to close.

Next Row: Sc 5 through both layers, sl st in the last st.

Fasten off, leaving a long tail for sewing.

Nose

With Rose Quartz.

Rnd 1: Sc 6 into a MR. (6 sts)

Rnd 2: Sc 2 in each st around. (12 sts)

Rnd 3: (Sc 1, sc 2 in next st) x6. (18 sts)

Rnd 4: Sc in each st around.

Rnd 5: (Sc 1, sc2tog) x6. (12 sts)

Fasten off, leaving a long tail for sewing.

Feet (make 2)

With Teak.

Rnd 1: Sc 6 into a MR. (6)

Rnd 2: Sc 2 in each st around. (12 sts)

Rnds 3–4: Sc in each st around.

The feet don't need to be stuffed. Flatten the opening of the foot and work the next round through both layers to close.

Next Row: Sc 5 through both layers, sl st in the last st.

Fasten off, leaving a long tail for sewing.

Beard

With White.

Ch 23.

Row 1: Hdc 3 in 3rd ch from hook, (hdc 3 in next ch) x11, sl st in next ch, (sl st in next ch, ch 14, hdc 3 in 3rd ch from hook, (hdc 3 in next ch) x11, sl st in next ch) x4.

Fasten off, leaving a long tail for sewing. Shape the 5 curls as needed.

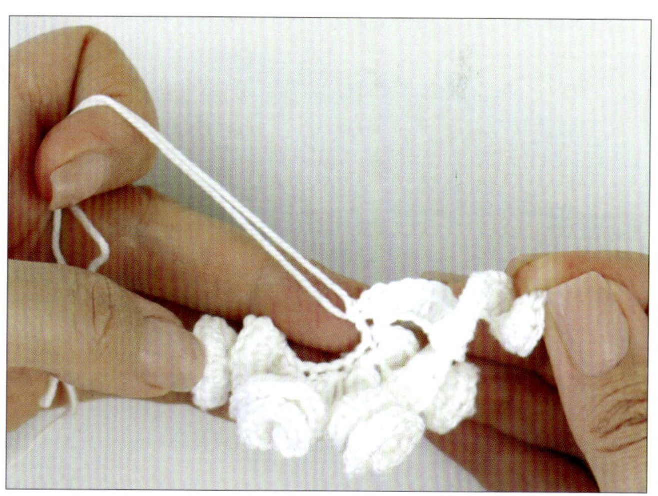

Boat Base (make 2)

With Brunet.

Ch 25.

Row 1: Sc in 2nd ch from hook, sc in next 23 ch, ch 1, turn. (24 sts)

Rows 2–22: Sc in each st across, ch 1, turn.

Row 23: Sc 11, sc2tog, sc 11, ch 1, turn. (23 sts)

Row 24: Sc in each st across, ch 1, turn.

Row 25: Sc 11, sc2tog, sc 10, ch 1, turn. (22 sts)

Row 26: Sc in each st across, ch 1, turn.

Row 27: Sc 10, sc2tog, sc 10, ch 1, turn. (21 sts)

Row 28: Sc in each st across, ch 1, turn.

Row 29: Sc 10, sc2tog, sc 9, ch 1, turn. (20 sts)

Row 30: Skip first st, sc 19, ch 1, turn. (19 sts)

Row 31: Skip first st, sc 18, ch 1, turn. (18 sts)

Row 32: Sc 8, sc2tog, sc 8, ch 1, turn. (17 sts)

Row 33: Skip first st, sc 16, ch 1, turn. (16 sts)

Row 34: Skip first st, sc 15 st, ch 1, turn. (15 sts)

Row 35: Sc 7, sc2tog, sc 6, ch 1, turn. (14 sts)

Row 36: Skip first st, sc 13, ch 1, turn. (13 sts)

Row 37: Skip first st, sc 12, ch 1, turn. (12 sts)

Row 38: Sc 5, sc2tog, sc 5, ch 1, turn. (11 sts)

Row 39: Skip first st, sc 10, ch 1, turn. (10 sts)

Row 40: Skip first st, sc 9, ch 1, turn. (9 sts)

Row 41: Sc 4, sc2tog, sc 3, ch 1, turn. (8 sts)

Row 42: Skip first st, sc 5, sc2tog, ch 1, turn. (6 sts)

Row 43: Skip first st, sc 3, sc2tog, ch 1, turn. (4 sts)

Row 44: (Sc2tog) x2. (2 sts)

Fasten off and weave in the yarn ends. Cut a piece of cardboard or plastic the shape of the base for reinforcement. If you use plastic, you can soften the edges with a nail file.

Make the second part same as the first but don't cut the yarn. Continue working in the next round through both layers to join the pieces.

Rnd 1: Sc 42 along one side of the bottoms, (sc, hdc, sc) in the corner, sc 22 along the straight edge, (sc, hdc, sc) in the corner, place the reinforcement inside the base, continue working through both layers, sc 42 along remaining side edge, sl st to close, don't turn. (112 sts)

Rnd 2: Ch 1, BL sc 2 in next st, BL sc 110, BL sc 2 in next st, sl st in first st to join. (114 sts)

Rnd 3: Ch 1, sc 2 in next st, sc 112, sc 2 in next st, sl st in first st to join. (116 sts)

Rnd 4: Ch 1, sc 2 in next st, sc 114, sc 2 in next st, sl st in first st to join. (118 sts)

Rnd 5: Ch 1, sc in each st around, sl st in first st to join.

Change to Navy Blue.

Rnd 6: Ch 1, sc in each st around, sl st in first st to join.

Change to Cardinal.

Rnd 7: Ch 1, sc in each st around, sl st in first st to join.

Change to Brunet.

Rnd 8: Ch 1, sc in each st around, sl st in first st to join.

Rnd 9: Ch 1, FL sc in each st around, sl st in first st to join.

Fasten off and weave in the yarn ends.

Mast

With Brunet.

Rnd 1: Sc 6 into a MR. (6 sts)

Rnds 2–49: Sc in each st around.

Fasten off, leaving a long tail.

Place a drop of glue on one of the ends of the skewer stick and insert it into the mast. Trim the excess length of the stick.

Sew the mast between Rows 28 and 30 of the inner base of the boat.

Sail

With White.

Ch 25.

Row 1: Sc in 2nd ch from hook, sc in next 23 ch, ch 1, turn. (24 sts)

Row 2: Sc in each st across, ch 1, turn.

Row 3: Sc 22, skip 1 st, sc in last st, ch 1, turn. (23 sts)

Rows 4–5: Sc 23, ch 1, turn.

Row 6: Skip first st, sc 22, ch 1, turn. (22 sts)

Rows 7–8: Sc in each st across, ch 1, turn.

Row 9: Sc 20, skip 1 st, sc in last st, ch 1, turn. (21 sts)

Row 10: Skip first st, sc 20, ch 1, turn. (20 sts)

Row 11: Sc 18, skip 1 st, sc in last st, ch 1, turn. (19 sts)

Row 12: Skip first st, sc 18, ch 1, turn. (18 sts)

Row 13: Sc 16, skip 1 st, sc in last st, ch 1, turn. (17 sts)

Row 14: Skip first st, sc 16, ch 1, turn. (16 sts)

Row 15: Sc 14, skip 1 st, sc in last st, ch 1, turn. (15 sts)

Row 16: Skip first st, sc 14 st, ch 1, turn. (14 sts)

Row 17: Sc 12, skip 1 st, sc in last st, ch 1, turn. (13 sts)

Row 18: Skip first st, sc 12, ch 1, turn. (12 sts)

Row 19: Sc 10, skip 1 st, sc in last st, ch 1, turn. (11 sts)

Row 20: Skip first st, sc 10, ch 1, turn. (10 sts)

Row 21: Sc 8, skip 1 st, sc in last st, ch 1, turn. (9 sts)

Row 22: Skip first st, sc 8, ch 1, turn. (8 sts)

Row 23: Sc 6, skip 1 st, sc in last st, ch 1, turn. (7 sts)

Row 24: Skip first st, sc 6, ch 1, turn. (6 sts)

Row 25: Sc 4, skip 1 st, sc in last st, ch 1, turn. (5 sts)

Row 26: Skip first st, sc 4, ch 1, turn. (4 sts)

Row 27: Sc 2, skip 1 st, sc in last st, ch 1, turn. (3 sts)

Row 28: Skip first st, sc 2, ch 1, turn. (2 sts)

Row 29: Sc2tog. (1 st)

Fasten off, leaving a long tail for sewing.

Flag

With Cardinal.

Ch 6.

Row 1: Sc in 2nd ch from hook, sc in next 4 ch, ch 1, turn. (5 sts)

Row 2: Sc in each st across, ch 1, turn.

Row 3: Skip first st, sc 4, ch 1, turn. (4 sts)

Row 4: Sc in each st across, ch 1, turn.

Row 5: Skip first st, sc 3, ch 1, turn. (3 sts)

Row 6: Sc in each st across, ch 1, turn.

Row 7: Skip first st, sc 2, ch 1, turn. (2 sts)

Row 8: Sc 2, ch 1, turn.

Row 9: Sc2tog. (1 st)

Fasten off, leaving a long tail for sewing.

Time to Put It All Together!

Sew the beard, centered between the eyes, between Rnds 5 and 7 of the head.

Stuff the nose and sew it, centered between the eyes, between Rnds 3 and 7 of the head.

Sew the arms to the sides of the robe, at Rnd 8 of the body, with 22 sts between them at the back.

Sew the feet to Rnd 1 at the bottom of the body, with 6 sts between them at the front.

Tie the sail and the flag to the mast, and hold them in place with a few sts.

SEWING GNOME

MATERIALS

Yarn

Yarn & Colors® 100% Mercerized Cotton (sport weight yarn) 1.75oz (50g)/137yds (125m)

Colors

Plum: 1.06oz (30g)/82yds (75m)
Clay: 0.35oz (10g)/27.3yds (25m)
Fuchsia: 0.35oz (10g)/27.3yds (25m)
Dark Pink: leftovers
Brunet: leftovers
Teak: leftovers
Limestone: leftovers
Pacific Blue: leftovers
Black: leftovers

- Size US 0 (2mm) crochet hook (you may need to go up/down based on your tension)
- Fiberfill
- 6mm black safety eyes
- Darning needle
- Locking stitch marker
- Scissors
- Pins

Gauge

7 stitches x 7 rounds in 1in/2.54cm

Let's Begin!

Hat

With Plum.

Rnd 1: Sc 6 into a MR. (6 sts)

Rnds 2–3: Sc in each st around.

Rnd 4: Sc 5, sc 2 in next st. (7 sts)

Rnd 5: Sc 6, sc 2 in next st. (8 sts)

Rnd 6: Sc 7, sc 2 in next st. (9 sts)

Rnd 7: Sc 8, sc 2 in next st. (10 sts)

Rnd 8: Sc 9, sc 2 in next st. (11 sts)

Rnd 9: Sc 10, sc 2 in next st. (12 sts)

Rnd 10: Sc in each st around.

Rnd 11: (Sc 2, sc 2 in next st) x4. (16 sts)

Rnd 12: Sc in each st around.

Rnd 13: (Sc 1, sc 2 in next st) x8. (24 sts)

Rnds 14–17: Sc in each st around.

Rnd 18: (Sc 2, sc 2 in next st) x8. (32 sts)

Rnds 19–20: Sc in each st around.

Rnd 21: (Sc 3, sc 2 in next st) x8. (40 sts)

Rnd 22: (Sc 9, sc 2 in next st) x4. (44 sts)

Rnd 23: (Sc 10, sc 2 in next st) x4. (48 sts)

Rnd 24: Sc in each st around.

Rnd 25: (Sc 7, sc 2 in next st) x6. (54 sts)

Rnd 26: Sc in each st around.

Rnd 27: (Sc 8, sc 2 in next st) x6. (60 sts)

Change to Fuchsia.

Rnds 28–29: Sc in each st around.

Change to Plum.

Rnd 30: (FL sc 9, FL sc 2 in next st) x6. (66 sts)

Rnd 31: Sc in each st around.

Rnd 32: (Sc 10, sc 2 in next st) x6. (72 sts)

Rnd 33: Sc in each st around.

Fasten off and weave in the yarn ends.

Head and Robe

With Clay.

Pull up a loop of Clay in any BL of Rnd 29 of the hat.

Rnd 1: BL sc in each st around. (60 sts)

Rnd 2: (Sc 8, sc2tog) x6. (54 sts)

Rnd 3: (Sc 7, sc2tog) x6. (48 sts)

Rnds 4–7: Sc in each st around.

Change to Plum.

Rnds 8–11: Sc in each st around.

Rnd 12: (Sc 7, sc 2 in next st) x6. (54 sts)

Rnds 13–16: Sc in each st around.

Place a locking marker in the loop while you make the face.

Position your gnome so that the held loop is centered at the back.

Insert safety eyes between Rnds 3 and 4 of the head, 10 sts apart.

Embroider the cheeks with Dark Pink.

Rnd 17: (Sc 8, sc 2 in next st) x6. (60 sts)

Rnds 18–20: Sc in each st around.

Rnd 21: (FL sc 9, FL sc 2 in next st) x6. (66 sts)

Rnd 22: Sc in each st around.

Rnd 23: (Sc 10, sc 2 in next st) x6. (72 sts)

Rnd 24: Sc in each st around.

Fasten off and weave in the yarn ends.

Bottom

Pull up a loop of Clay in the BL of any st of Rnd 20 of the robe.

Rnd 1: (BL sc 8, BL sc2tog) x6. (54 sts)

Rnd 2: (Sc 7, sc2tog) x6. (48 sts)

Rnd 3: (Sc 4, sc2tog) x8. (40 sts)

Rnd 4: (Sc 3, sc2tog) x8. (32 sts)

Rnd 5: (Sc 2, sc2tog) x8. (24 sts)

Stuff the body.

Rnd 6: (Sc 1, sc2tog) x8. (16 sts)

Rnd 7: (Sc2tog) x8. (8 sts)

Fasten off, leaving a long tail. Using a darning needle, weave the yarn tail through the FL of each st of last rnd. Pull tight to close. Weave in the yarn end.

Arms (make 2)

With Clay.

Rnd 1: Sc 6 into a MR. (6 sts)

Rnd 2: Sc 2 in each st around. (12 sts)

Rnds 3–4: Sc in each st around.

Change to Plum.

Rnds 5–12: Sc in each st around.

Lightly stuff the arm. Flatten the opening of the arm and work the next row through both layers to close.

Next Row: Sc 5 through both layers, sl st in the last st.

Fasten off, leaving a long tail for sewing.

Nose

With Clay.

Rnd 1: Sc 6 into a MR. (6 sts)

Rnd 2: Sc 2 in each st around. (12 sts)

Rnd 3: (Sc 1, sc 2 in next st) x6. (18 sts)

Rnd 4: Sc in each st around.

Rnd 5: (Sc 1, sc2tog) x6. (12 sts)

Fasten off, leaving a long tail for sewing.

Feet (make 2)

With Teak.

Rnd 1: Sc 6 into a MR. (6 sts)

Rnd 2: Sc 2 in each st around. (12 sts)

Rnds 3–4: Sc in each st around.

The feet don't need to be stuffed. Flatten the opening of the foot and work the next row through both layers to close.

Next Row: Sc 5 through both layers, sl st in the last st.

Fasten off, leaving a long tail for sewing.

Bow

With Fuchsia.

Ch 6.

Row 1: Sc in 2nd ch from hook, sc in 4 ch, ch 1, turn. (5 sts)

Rows 2–18: Sc 5, ch 1, turn.

Row 19: Sc 5.

Fold the bow in half, and work the next row through both layers to create a circle.

Row 20: Sl st 5 through both layers.

Fasten off, leaving a long yarn tail. Wind the tails around the center of the bow a few times to squeeze it together and make a knot. Leave a long tail for sewing.

Braid Tips (make 2)

With Brunet.

Rnd 1: Leaving a long tail, sc 6 into a MR. (6 sts)

Rnd 2: Sc 2 in each st around. (12 sts)

Rnds 3–4: Sc in each st around.

The tip doesn't need to be stuffed.

Rnd 5: (Sc2tog) x6. (6 sts)

Rnd 6: (Sc2tog) x3. (3 sts)

Fasten off, leaving a long tail for sewing.

Braids (make 2)

With Brunet.

Ch 18.

Row 1: Sc in 2nd ch from hook, sc in next 14 ch, sl st in next ch, ch 16, sc in 2nd ch from hook, sc in next 14 ch, sl st in next ch, ch 16, sc in 2nd ch from hook, sc in next 14 ch.

Fasten off, leaving a long tail for sewing. Holding the end down with a pin, braid the 3 strands together. Sew the braid tip to this end. Twist a length of Fuchsia around the join a few times.

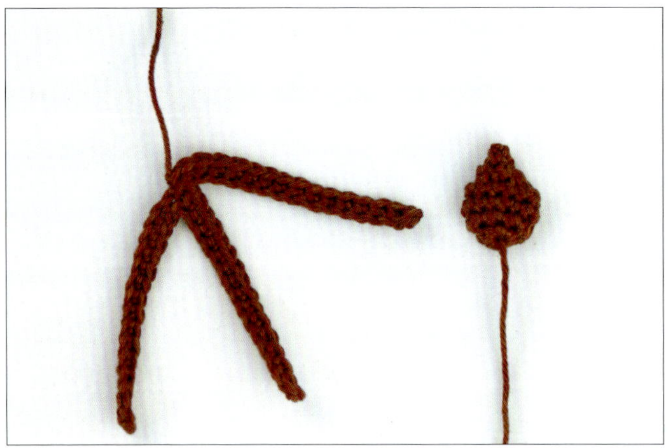

Spool of Thread

With Limestone.

Rnd 1: Sc 6 into a MR. (6 sts)

Rnd 2: Sc 2 in each st around. (12 sts)

Rnd 3: (Sc 1, sc 2 in next st) x6. (18 sts)

Rnd 4: (Sc 2, sc 2 in next st) x6. (24 sts)

Rnd 5: BL sc in each st around.

Rnd 6: (BL sc 2, BL sc2tog) x6. (18 sts)

Rnds 7–14: Sc in each st around.

Rnd 15: (FL sc 2, FL sc 2 in next st) x6. (24 sts)

Rnd 16: BL sc in each st around.

Lightly stuff.

Rnd 17: (BL sc 2 st, BL sc2tog) x6. (18 sts)

Rnd 18: (Sc 1, sc2tog) x6. (12 sts)

Rnd 19: (Sc2tog) x6. (6 sts)

Fasten off, leaving a long tail. Using a darning needle, weave the yarn tail through the FL of each st of last rnd. Pull tight to close. Weave in the yarn end. Wind a strand of yarn around the center of the spool several times.

Scissors

With Pacific Blue.

Rnd 1: Sc 6 into a MR. (6 sts)

Rnds 2–11: Sc in each st around.

The scissors don't need to be stuffed. Flatten the opening of the scissors and work the next row through both layers to close.

Next Row: Sc 3 through both layers, ch 22, sl st in each ch, sl st in next st of row, ch 22, sl st in each ch, sl st in next st of row. Fasten off and leave a yarn tail.

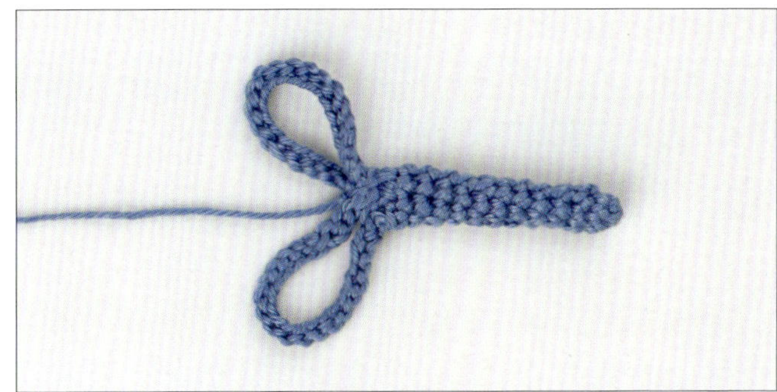

Using a darning needle, sew together 3 sts of both loops to form the handles. Weave in the yarn end. Using Black, make some sts at Rnd 11 to simulate the screw.

Time to Put It All Together!

Sew the braids to Rnd 1 at the sides of the head, with 19 sts between them at the front.

Stuff the nose and sew it, centered between the eyes and between Rnds 3 and 7 of the head.

Sew the bow on one side of the hat between Rnds 28 and 29.

Sew the arms to the sides of the robe, at Rnd 8, with 22 sts between them at the back.

Sew the feet to Rnd 1 at the bottom of the body, with 6 sts between them at the front.

SWIMMING GNOME

MATERIALS

Yarn

Yarn & Colors® 100% Mercerized Cotton (sport weight yarn) 1.75oz (50g)/137yds (125m)

Colors

Pacific Blue: 0.35oz (10g)/27.3yds (25m)
Limestone: 0.35oz (10g)/27.3yds (25m)
Raspberry: 0.71oz (20g)/54.7yds (50m)
Dark Pink: leftovers
Sunflower: 0.71oz (20g)/54.7yds (50m)
Nordic Blue: leftovers
Navy Blue: leftovers
Teak: leftovers
Orange: leftovers
Black: leftovers

- Size US 0 (2mm) crochet hook (you may need to go up/down based on your tension)
- Fiberfill
- 6mm black safety eyes
- Darning needle
- Locking stitch marker
- Scissors
- Pins

Gauge

7 stitches x 7 rounds in 1in/2.54cm

Let's Begin!

Cap

With Pacific Blue.

Rnd 1: Sc 6 into a MR. (6 sts)

Rnd 2: Sc 2 in each st around. (12 sts)

Rnd 3: (Sc 1, sc 2 in next st) x6. (18 sts)

Rnd 4: (Sc 2, sc 2 in next st) x6. (24 sts)

Rnd 5: (Sc 3, sc 2 in next st) x6. (30 sts)

Rnd 6: (Sc 4, sc 2 in next st) x6. (36 sts)

Rnd 7: (Sc 5, sc 2 in next st) x6. (42 sts)

Rnd 8: (Sc 6, sc 2 in next st) x6. (48 sts)

Rnd 9: (Sc 7, sc 2 in next st) x6. (54 sts)

Rnds 10–13: Sc in each st around.

Rnd 14: (Sc 8, sc 2 in next st) x6. (60 sts)

Rnd 15: Sc in each st around.

Rnd 16: FL sc in each st around.

Rnds 17–19: Sc in each st around.

Fasten off and weave in the yarn ends.

Head and Robe

With Limestone.

Pull up a loop of Limestone in BL at center back of Rnd 15 of the cap.

Rnd 1: BL sc in each st around. (60 sts)

Rnd 2: (Sc 8, sc2tog) x6. (54 sts)

Rnd 3: (Sc 7, sc2tog) x6. (48 sts)

Rnds 4–7: Sc in each st around.

Change to Raspberry.

Rnds 8–11: Sc in each st around.

Rnd 12: (Sc 7, sc 2 in next st) x6. (54 sts)

Rnds 13–16: Sc in each st around.

Place a locking marker in the loop while you make the face.

Position your gnome so that the held loop is centered at the back.

Insert safety eyes between Rnds 3 and 4 of the head, 10 sts apart.

Embroider the cheeks with Dark Pink.

Rnd 17: (Sc 8, sc 2 in next st) x6. (60 sts)

Rnds 18–20: Sc in each st around.

Rnd 21: (FL sc 9, FL sc 2 in next st) x6. (66 sts)

Rnd 22: Sc in each st around.

Rnd 23: (Sc 10, sc 2 in next st) x6. (72 sts)

Rnd 24: Sc in each st around.

Fasten off and weave in the yarn ends.

Bottom

Pull up a loop of Limestone in the BL of any st of Rnd 20 of the robe.

Rnd 21: (BL sc 8, BL sc2tog) x6. (54 sts)

Rnd 22: (Sc 7, sc2tog) x6. (48 sts)

Rnd 23: (Sc 4, sc2tog) x8. (40 sts)

Rnd 24: (Sc 3, sc2tog) x8. (32 sts)

Rnd 25: (Sc 2, sc2tog) x8. (24 sts)

Stuff the body.

Rnd 26: (Sc 1, sc2tog) x8. (16 sts)

Rnd 27: (Sc2tog) x8. (8 sts)

Fasten off, leaving a long tail. Using a darning needle, weave the yarn tail through the FL of each st of the last rnd. Pull tight to close. Weave in the yarn end.

Arms (make 2)

With Limestone.

Rnd 1: Sc 6 into a MR. (6 sts)

Rnd 2: Sc 2 in each st around. (12 sts)

Rnds 3–4: Sc in each st around.

Change to Raspberry.

Rnds 5–12: Sc in each st around.

Lightly stuff the arm. Flatten the opening of the arm and work the next row through both layers to close.

Next Row: Sc 5 through both layers, sl st in last st.

Fasten off, leaving a long tail for sewing.

Nose

With Limestone.

Rnd 1: Sc 6 into a MR. (6 sts)

Rnd 2: Sc 2 in each st around. (12 sts)

Rnd 3: (Sc 1, sc 2 in next st) x6. (18 sts)

Rnd 4: Sc in each st around.

Rnd 5: (Sc 1, sc2tog) x6. (12 sts)

Fasten off, leaving a long tail for sewing.

Feet (make 2)

With Teak.

Rnd 1: Sc 6 into a MR. (6 sts)

Rnd 2: Sc 2 in each st around. (12 sts)

Rnds 3–4: Sc in each st around.

The feet don't need to be stuffed. Flatten the opening of the foot and work the next row through both layers to close.

Next Row: Sc 5 through both layers, sl st in last st.

Fasten off, leaving a long tail for sewing.

Goggles

With Nordic Blue.

Lenses (make 2)

Rnd 1: Sc 6 into a MR. (6 sts)

Rnd 2: Sc 2 in each st around. (12 sts)

Fasten off and weave in the yarn end.

Join the Lenses.

With Navy Blue pick up a loop in any st of one of the lenses.

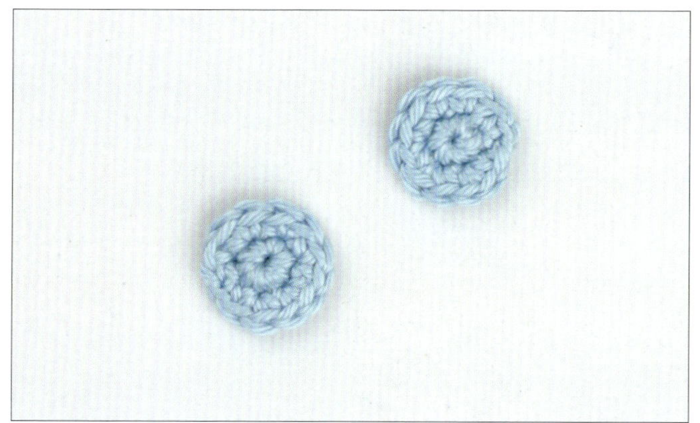

Rnd 3: (Sc 1, sc 2 in next st) x6, ch 3, (sc in next st, sc 2 in next st) x6 in the second lens, sc 3 in ch between lenses, sl st in first st of the rnd. Fasten off and weave in the yarn end. Make a ch 46 sts long. Sew an end to each side of the goggles.

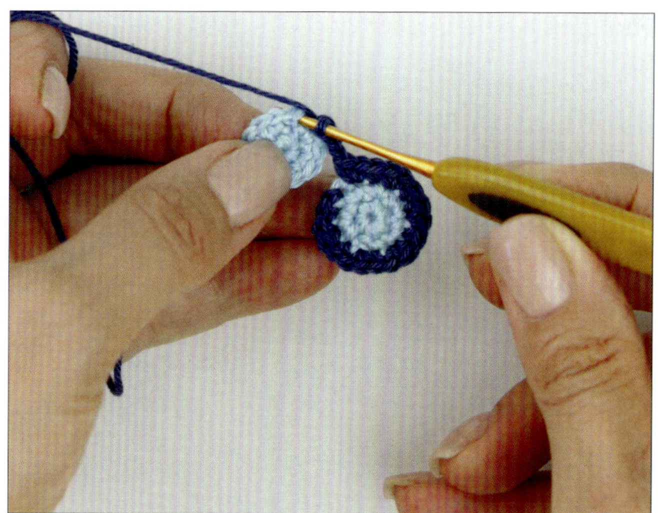

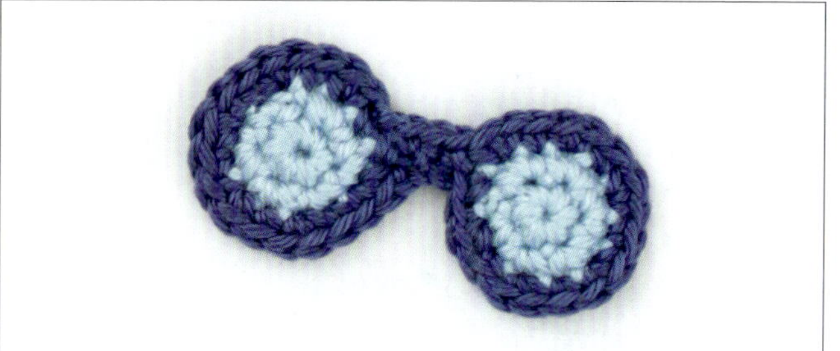

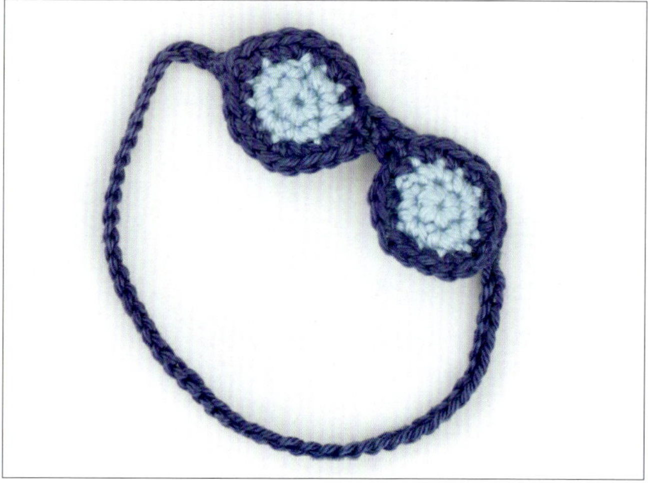

Floatie

With Sunflower. Stuff the floatie as you go.

Rnd 1: Sc 6 into a MR. (6 sts)

Rnd 2: Sc 2 in each st around. (12 sts)

Rnds 3–80: Sc in each st around.

Fasten off, leaving a long tail for sewing. Sew the ends of the floatie together.

Duck Head

With Sunflower.

Rnd 1: Sc 6 into a MR. (6 sts)

Rnd 2: Sc 2 in each st around. (12 sts)

Rnd 3: (Sc 1, sc 2 in next st) x6. (18 sts)

Rnd 4: (Sc 2, sc 2 in next st) x6. (24 sts)

Rnd 5: (Sc 3, sc 2 in next st) x6. (30 sts)

Rnds 6–11: Sc in each st around.

Rnd 12: (Sc 3, sc2tog) x6. (24 sts)

Rnd 13: (Sc 2, sc2tog) x6. (18 sts)

Rnd 14: (Sc 1, sc2tog) x6. (12 sts)

Stuff the head.

Rnd 15: (Sc2tog) x6. (6 sts)

Fasten off, leaving a long tail. Using a darning needle, weave the yarn tail through the FL of each st of the last rnd. Pull tight to close. Leave a long tail for sewing.

Beak

With Orange.

Ch 4.

Rnd 1: Sc 2 in 2nd ch from hook, sc in next ch, sc 3 in next ch, continue along other side of foundation ch, sc in next ch, sc 2 in next ch. (9 sts)

Rnd 2: Sc 2 in next st, sc 3, sc 2 in next st, sc 4. (11 sts)

Rnd 3: Sc in each st around.

Fasten off, leaving a long tail for sewing.

Assembling the Floatie

With Black, embroider the eyes on Rnd 8 of the duck head, with 6 sts between. Sew the beak, centered between the eyes, on Rnd 10 of the duck head. Sew the duck head to the top of the floatie.

Time to Put It All Together!

Stuff the nose and sew it, centered between the eyes and between Rnds 3 and 7 of the head.

Sew the goggles on the cap.

Sew the arms to the sides of the robe on Rnd 8, with 22 sts between them at the back.

Sew the feet to Rnd 1 at the bottom of the body, with 6 sts between them at the front.

Place the floatie on the body.